DISOBEDIENCE

a novel

Daniel Sarah Karasik

Book*hug Press
Toronto 2024

Library and Archives Canada Cataloguing in Publication

Title: Disobedience / Daniel Sarah Karasik.
Names: Karasik, Daniel, 1986- author.
Identifiers: Canadiana (print) 20230571115 | Canadiana (ebook) 20230571131
  ISBN 9781771668972 (softcover)
  ISBN 9781771668958 (EPUB)
Classification: LCC PS8621.A6224 D57 2024 | DDC C813/.6—dc23

The production of this book was made possible through the generous assistance of the Canada Council for the Arts and the Ontario Arts Council. Book*hug Press also acknowledges the support of the Government of Canada through the Canada Book Fund and the Government of Ontario through the Ontario Book Publishing Tax Credit and the Ontario Book Fund.

Book*hug Press acknowledges that the land on which we operate is the traditional territory of many nations, including the Mississaugas of the Credit, the Anishnabeg, the Chippewa, the Haudenosaunee, and the Wendat peoples. We recognize the enduring presence of many diverse First Nations, Inuit, and Métis peoples, and are grateful for the opportunity to meet and work on this territory.

INSIDE

OUTFOX THE JAILERS: GET TO COME. SUCH AS ON this morning, when Shael learns—via the pale green letters of their bedroom wall's infoscreen—that the motor assembly trainer is ill. The trainees will be left under the supervision of the surveillance unit, a black glass dome lodged discreetly in one corner of the ceiling. *We would like to remind you that attendance is mandatory and delinquency will be severely punished*, the infoscreen instructs. But Shael knows the surveillance footage won't be reviewed until the evening, leaving time to alert and secure sign-off from Guard 937, with whom Coe has a delicate arrangement.

Shael passes their message to Coe through Guard 3476, with whom Shael has a similar arrangement, when 3476 arrives with rations. Just a single word: *medic*. Which will let Coe know to meet at their typical hour (they rendezvous every time this trainer is out—often enough) in the indefinitely under-renovation wing of Infirmary Seven. There might be another unlicensed couple there, or several: the place is known to those with need to know it. Some might be guards in disguise, or informants. A serious risk, and far from the only risk involved. Surveillance units aren't activated in the abandoned infirmary wing, at least not noticeably, but they track the whole route there.

Potenza, Shael's mother, calls them to eat. They sit with their younger siblings in the dwelling hub's common room, boxy and beige and barely furnished.

"You're eating quickly," Potenza says.

"Running late," Shael says, not lifting their eyes from their plate.

"He wants to see his girlfriend," says Mertia, the smallest. Among Shael's kin, only Potenza knows they're not a *he*.

Mertia's giggles infect Vinsan, her brother, two years older, who seldom smiles anymore. Potenza eats, impassive, reaches over to brush Shael's long, wavy hair out of their eyes. "How can you see," she murmurs.

In the shadows of their grey bedroom, a windowless concrete cave, Shael dresses for Coe. The black thong Coe likes; the white corset with delicate pink snaps. Lips stained just a shade or three redder than normal, no sure indication of Betweenness, plausibly deniable. A subtle effect also with the lash shade, though here discretion is harder to achieve, requiring a light touch with the application brush, lest clumping make it impossible to credibly feign innocence if scrutinized by guards, to bat dramatic lashes and say: *What? They're just like that.* Standard masculine robe worn over their corset, gown hidden in their satchel. Risky...but what are they to do, not live? Accept the tedium of a life planned and controlled in every detail? Let the corporation cow them out of every delight besides the easy, deathly high of Sanem?

At hub unlock, Shael files out as usual. They follow the crowded route to training. Down the turquoise corridors of the hub block, painted generations ago like all the other blocks, supposedly to make confinement less oppressive, lower the suicide rate—then extraordinarily high, even by the camp's standards. The effect has been to turn each journey into a fever dream. Shael never gets fully used to it, though they've never known anywhere else. Paint has peeled off all over the place, leaving even the brightest corridors grey-dappled. Silence rules here, broken only by the swish of regulation robes. There was once music in the corridors, a haunting of ancient song, but it filled participants with such melancholy—an affliction disastrous for productivity, the assessors noted—that it was removed.

Shael moves in step with the mass of other participants, along a narrow lane, its boundary marked on the floor in white. There's no

explicit penalty for stepping over that white line, but so well-disciplined
are most of Flint's participants, so thick the atmospheric threat of punishment at all times, that the lane holds its traffic as sternly as if its verge
were made of steel. No participant meets eyes with any other. No one
speaks. A spectacle of perfect obedience, in which Shael participates
as seamlessly as possible—so as to more invisibly escape it. How many
of the others walking alongside them feel and do the same? Maybe a
greater number than their overseers would guess.

At the checkpoint between hub blocks, Shael flashes their iden-
tification papers: trainee, reporting to 9877C. The bored guard on
duty sweeps them along, just one participant among the dull many.
Through the orange corridors of the next block, past metal door after
metal door, behind each of them a dwelling hub housing several families. In the early days, Flint experimented with different forms of gen-
erational housing, but the model placing children with at least one of
their birth parents was found to have advantages for social control that
just couldn't be matched. Parents and children would reliably impose
a certain discipline on each other: the parents moderating their own
risks for their children's sake, while pressuring their young to avoid
attracting attention. Potenza, for instance, who's known about Shael's
Betweenness for as long as Shael can remember, has always policed her
child's gender with more worried vigilance than any official agency
could do. Surveilling them, chastising them for transgressive play,
urging them to conform: to keep them safe, ostensibly, but also doing
the corporation's work of social pacification for it. As do the children
who torment peers thought to be Betweens. And the withholding of
intimate match licences from participants suspected of such deviance.
And the hard correction centres.

The active entrance to Infirmary Seven is a reinforced glass door,
located in the main passage of a hub block painted a soft purple, 9876C.
Behind this door, Shael knows, lies a vast, gleaming clinic. All steel and
glass, equipment of the latest design, medical minds of verified high
competence—here the corporation spares no effort. Trin, a young
participant frequently in fragile health, has told Shael all about it. Has

described how whenever Magent, the corporation that controls the continent's lands south of the Waste, sends diplomatic missions to Flint's camp, Flint executives make sure to work a tour of the medical facilities into the visit. *Why go to such trouble?* the Magent people ask. *Why bother with this healing of bodies that are mostly interchangeable and anyway are reproducing above the population replacement rate?* (Magent's camp is said to be unimaginably hellish.) According to Trin, who relates her insights dispassionately, the analysis of a person from whom pain has stripped illusions, Flint justifies its oases of bodily care in a couple of ways. First, simply, it's convenient to employ bodies that work in as optimized and normalized a state as possible. Second, and more important, a strategic investment in certain narrow forms of care makes it harder for agitators among participants to frame the corporation as unkind. Flint manages its camp by an old paternal logic: the corporation protects and provides, it does so effectively in a dangerous world where such protection and provision is needed, so its domination is legitimate and must be accepted by those it rules. That it also rules by force—of course nobody has a *choice* about their confinement—is beside the point.

Shael passes Infirmary Seven's active entrance without a glance. They continue down the hall till they reach a plain metal door, unnumbered but otherwise identical to those that lead to dwelling hubs. Without a break in their step, resisting the perverse urge to glance over their shoulder at the nearest surveillance unit, they open the door and slip through. As always, they marvel not only at finding the door unlocked, but also at how *unremarkable* it is to discover it that way, so abundant are the gaps in Flint's supposedly seamless matrix of control. How is it possible that the more rules, surveillance, and threats of correction proliferate, the more air pockets of freedom appear as well? The corporation, Shael thinks, delivers on some of its propaganda's promises despite itself. In films screened on the compulsory celebration days each month, a narrating voice claims that Flint's vast prison camp ("supported life/work zone") offers prisoners ("participants") maximal freedom by relieving them of the burden of constant decision making, while imposing on them a healthful discipline. The corporation's real designs, of course, can be read off the calluses of Potenza's fingers, sewing for most of the hours she's awake: the virtually limitless labour power of a captive workforce, sweating for the Mountainers' benefit. Yet carelessness, laziness, desire among the guards, who, prisoners themselves, are treated little better than the rest, supply liberties Flint never meant to offer. Sign-off on compromising surveillance footage. An unlocked door.

Unlike the officially occupied section of the infirmary, the abandoned wing is glassless. Steel surfaces, grey walls. Scaffolding lines the halls, illumined with a faint blue glow. No one in sight. Not far from where Coe will be waiting, there's a small examination room without a door. Shael ducks into the room and squirms out of their loose robe, withdraws the form-fitting gown from their satchel. Before they can pull it on, there's a disturbance nearby. Voices, shuffling. Shael freezes, naked apart from underwear and corset. They flatten their back against the wall, watch the corridor. Two bodies drift into view. Muffled giggles, a kiss. Two feminine-appearing people, absorbed in each other. They're gone as soon as they appear. Shael exhales, dresses.

Coe is waiting in the examination room next door. Palpably impatient, hungry for Shael when they arrive. Yet also preoccupied, not fully present behind his eyes.

"What is it?" Shael asks.

"The group's dance," Coe replies.

"Is something wrong?"

"Just delays," Coe says. "The usual. Nothing worth talking about."

He slides off the examination table where he's been perched, squeezes Shael's waist with his long, slender hands. Coe has no need to specify that by "the group" he means the clandestine revolutionary organization called the Blood Moon, doesn't have to explain that "dance" refers to a planned attack on a correctors' station, because Shael knows Coe's codes. And Coe knows Shael. Knows, for instance, that if he slaps Shael's bum, hard, and maintains a stern demeanour—steely as a corrector—Shael will let out a short, sharp cry, which they'll promptly swallow, trying to regain their composure.

"Also safer for everyone if I don't say more," Coe goes on, and Shael nods and opens their mouth to reply, but then they're on their knees and their mouth is occupied.

The sounds of lips and tongue on skin are muted, absorbed by the walls of the examination room. The door is locked behind them. Rare privacy. Shael's eyes trace Coe, lean and strong, his height exaggerated by the angle. A mountain of boy.

"Do you need correcting?" Coe asks, in precisely the tone of a corrector humiliating a participant.

Shael eases their mouth free just enough to whisper, with a melodic mischief that, in the language they and Coe alone share, confirms permission: "Never."

Coe returns Shael's mouth to its task, not gently.

Shael squeaks.

"I've seen you sneaking across hub blocks that aren't yours," Coe says. "Delinquent from training. Entering forbidden areas. You've done it multiple times now." He runs his fingers through Shael's thick chestnut waves. "If I report this delinquency, now an established pattern, you're likely to get more than a whipping. More than even a public whipping. You may be sent down to a centre."

Shael groans a word that might be *no*.

"The latest executives' meeting concluded that discipline has been slipping, we've become far too lenient. If I report you, you'll be made an example." Coe speeds up. "Unless we do this differently. Unless I correct you here myself."

Coe grabs Shael by the upper arm, lifts them to their feet, and bends them over the examination table. With a swift efficiency that always surprises Shael no matter how many times they do this kind of scene, Coe tears open the fasteners on Shael's gown, rolls its lower half up to their waist, smacks their bum once, and yanks their underwear down to their knees.

Shael trembles. Their clit, hard, presses against the examination table.

"You prefer that I correct you myself, yes?" asks Coe.

"Yes," Shael whispers.

"You participants, you're given everything," Coe murmurs, riffling through his satchel. "All your needs are satisfied in our supported life/ work zone, yet you conduct yourselves like spoiled, ungrateful children." He pulls out a correction paddle, the kind found in every dwelling hub per regulation: a dense, translucent plastic oval with a rubber handle.

When Coe gives Shael a first hard smack, Shael feels as if their whole bum has been transformed into an angry bruise. A sob springs to their throat. Yet they know, from long familiarity with such implements, that if they were to glance at their bottom now it would look, at worst, a little pink.

"That hurts, doesn't it," Coe says.

"Hurts a lot," Shael rasps.

Another stroke lands, harder than the last. Shael cries out.

"That wasn't an invitation to whine about it," Coe says. He beats Shael several more times in quick succession.

Shael yelps without echo, and in a fugitive moment of thought between flares of pain, they wonder whether these walls were built to entomb other screams. But it's impossible to dwell on such thoughts for long. Blows land without respite, absorbing all Shael's attention.

"Good, you *should* whimper," says Coe, not letting up. "Maybe that means you're learning. Maybe you're beginning to grasp the virtue of obedience." *Smack.* "That's what we value in a Flint participant, Shael Potenza-brood 9872A." *Smack.* "Obedience. Do you understand?"

"Y-yes."

"We ask so little of you. We ask only." *Smack.* "That you." *Smack.* "Obey."

Coe swings hard, connects. Shael moans.

"Obey and this doesn't have to happen. Obey and your every need will be provided for. Obey and life can be so easy. Why do you insolent little ones insist on making your own lives so difficult?"

Shael doesn't know whether they can take much more. But just then Coe pauses and goes to his satchel, returning with the items he's filched from his brother, now two years into a licensed match. A barrier, lubrication. Shael unbends and pivots to face Coe, meets his gaze.

"Did I say you could stand up?" Coe says.

"Kiss me," Shael says. They can feel their lash shade has run.

Coe kisses them, stops abruptly, gives Shael's face a light, sharp slap. "You think you're in charge now?"

Shael bends forward, reaches back, spreads their cheeks. "Yes."

And at this point, as usual, Coe drops the scene, becomes again just a lover who cares for Shael and wants them to feel good, who looks at Shael as if they're made of a sweetness deeper than Sanem. But in Shael's mind, secretly, the scene continues as they're fucked. In their mind they're still being corrected. They've never yet confessed this particular inflection of fantasy to Coe, have never let on that they experience penetration, too, as a punishment, and that feeling this way makes sex good for them, makes sex sex. But it does. Overwhelmingly it does.

"Do you think we're broken," they ask Coe afterwards, as the two lie together on the examination table, examining each other. "Do you think it's ugly to do this the way we do?"

"Which way?"

"With violence."

"It isn't violence if we both want it."

"But to make sex out of...the camp. Correction."

"What else is it good for," Coe says. "If we can't make pleasure from it."

"I don't understand how I want this so much." They bury their face in his neck. "To be corrected by you. I think about it so much. When I'm so scared of it happening for real."

"Because you know I'd never really harm you."

"Am I still red?" They crane around to look.

"Barely."

"That's the cruellest thing about the correction paddles. All that pain and nothing to show for it."

"They made them that way on purpose," Coe says. "They want us to feel like any time we're screaming, we're overreacting. We're just being babies. *Look, hardly a mark. What are you crying about?*" He runs his fingers through Shael's hair. "But we're not overreacting."

Shael pictures hands in Coe's hair. Not their own hands, not caressing, but larger, rougher hands, yanking, dragging: the first time Shael saw Coe, as he was being hauled away from training for correction. It took four guards and a corrector, the latter conducting Coe out of the training hall by his scalp. Coe had sabotaged a week's worth of starsugar cakes on the training floor. The corrector whipped him in the next room so all the other trainees could hear his screams. Afterwards, the officials shoved him back into the hall, naked, his backside and thighs covered in red stripes. Clearly more than a correction paddle had been used. And indeed the corrector who followed close behind him, a massive man reputed to be even more sadistic than the others, was holding a switch. As it had done many times before, the sight of a switch struck Shael as surreal. Not because it made vivid the cruelty of the camp—routine from childhood—but because it was one of the few objects within Flint's carceral realm that weren't synthetic. Because the switch in the corrector's hand, the tool of torment he'd used to reduce a strong, defiant boy to limping frailty, had been introduced to the camp from the world beyond it. *Because it came from a tree.* So on the first day Shael saw Coe, Shael saw Coe weep. And they thought: *I would heal him, if he'd let me.* Take the pain of his punishment, even. Translate it into their own body and return his strength to him, which he would need for the revenge he must now take.

Coe was sent back to the starsugar cake trainee line and watched closely. But, as always, surveillance had its gaps. When the group was granted a latrine break, Shael filed out just behind Coe. Lips close to the tall boy's nape, they murmured: "That looked like it hurt. I'm sorry." Coe gave a subtle start but didn't turn. "They'll regret it later," he whispered. "You're stronger than they are," Shael said, "it's obvious." Almost imperceptibly—discreet black glass domes watched them even when the guards didn't—Coe tilted his head. Shael went on: "You should be correcting *them*." Coe half turned to face them. Caught himself, stopped. The nerve of Shael's flirtation, if that's what it was, was astonishing. If they were overheard, the consequences would be brutal.

They filed into the latrine hall. No privacy there, hardly enough space for all the trainees to use the waterwall at once. Even if neither of them had intended it, Shael's and Coe's shoulders would have touched. "I hate standing like this," Shael murmured. "With the men." Did the tall boy understand? Coe whispered back: "You're right…I should be correcting them. But not just individuals. I'm going to correct the whole system." *Don't look at his cock don't look at his cock don't look at his—* "How do you train to be that kind of corrector?" Shael asked, eyes fixed straight ahead, mostly. "Is there a training stream?" Coe shook out whatever it was he held in his hand, from which Shael averted their gaze as if it were the sun. "Certainly," Coe said. "But no assessor or trainer will tell you about it." Both of them adjusted their robes at the same time. Their hands brushed. "That kind of training… you get it from your fellow trainees. A lateral education." Coe glanced at the others near them. The few within earshot of whispers appeared to be paying them no attention. "It's too bad," said Coe, "they still haven't reopened that wing of Infirmary Seven. You know the one?" Shael blinked. They did know. "Too bad," Shael agreed. "What if someone fell ill on the way home from tonight's trainee group meal," they went on. "Would the other wings have capacity for them?" Coe's face gave nothing away. "Maybe not."

Always the same examination room, in the same pale blue light. As often as they could manage. Always at risk of beatings or worse if they were caught, dark joyless versions of acts made joyful when they turned them into play, together, by choice. "Tell you a secret," Coe once whispered to Shael, the two of them wrapped around each other, out of breath. "Nearly everyone I've been with has wanted to be corrected, at least a little. Not corrected for real, I mean. But the way we do it." Coe had stolen away with many partners, of many genders. When he'd realized his participant approval score was too poor for him ever to be granted a licensed match, he'd decided to just go ahead and follow his desire wherever it led. And his cratered approval score resulted in work assignments so low-trust—menial, undersupervised in practice—that he could often find a way to shirk them. "I like this kind of correcting," he went on, "so it's nice that the desire for it is so common. But it also *annoys* me that it's so common, because it feels like another way that people here make peace with the horror. Instead of working together to destroy it." Tracing circles on Coe's back with their fingers, Shael murmured: "It's possible to want both. To do both." Coe kissed their forehead. "There's only one of you in the whole camp." Shael kissed his lips, said: "You're special too." A tension in the set of Coe's jaw. "Not special," he said. "Just angry."

Yet Coe's anger has also been his fuel, Shael knows. Has driven his work in the Blood Moon, animated his hunger to understand the camp and the world beyond it. He's described how, as a child, he raced through the titles in the licensed library cart and, enraged by its limitations, demanded to know more. His mother secured access to an unlicensed knowledge network, as Shael's mother did also, committed to nurturing their bright children's curiosity. It's believed that the texts in the unlicensed knowledge networks are smuggled into the camp from the mountains. The participants who manage the networks alter the text covers to be indistinguishable from licensed items, and the texts themselves tend not to be outright seditious: while some are overtly political, many purport to be more straightforwardly historical, giving descriptive life to rumours of antiquity, such as seas in which a person could safely swim. So it's rare that possession of such texts is discovered or punished. But not unheard of. Every so often, word gets around that some forbidden literary artifact, a comic adventure or tract about Betweens, has been found in a child's bedroom, and the whole family whipped or sent to a hard correction centre. Such stories seem plausible enough, because every day in the camp, in ways large and small, curiosity is treated with severity.

"They're terrified of our curiosity because they know if it were set free, the camp could never contain it," Coe says now, still running his fingers through Shael's hair. The two have been in the abandoned infirmary wing for nearly an hour. Shael needs to leave soon to get to their next training module, where the trainer is unlikely to be absent. "They don't want us to develop a clear mental picture of the world outside. They figure that if we knew what we're missing, we'd either go mad or revolt. Or both."

Shael runs their fingertips over their nipples absently. Though still small—small enough to hide as necessary, for the most part—their breasts have grown more rapidly in the past year, the areolas widening. They've been taking endos more consistently. Reckless, some would say. With changes written on their body, they could so easily be caught. "Can you picture it? The outside? When I try to, I feel like I'm trusting the texts too much. Have you ever wondered whether maybe the camp controls even the unlicensed texts? Maybe the assessors have screened everything we've ever read."

"Or written the texts themselves. Yes."

"So how are we supposed to believe any report of what's out there? Maybe there's nothing. Besides executives in airlock domes."

Coe slides his hands over theirs, cups their breasts. "There are circuits of knowledge that the assessors don't know about. Not recorded in any texts."

"Sometimes I find it hard to believe there's anything they don't know about. Even us, here. Maybe they let us rebel like this because it doesn't actually threaten them. As soon as it does, we're dead."

Coe sits up, props his back against the wall. "It's possible they know. Either way, we'll never be safe here."

"So what are we supposed to do? I'm not as brave as you, I hate knowing that everything I want could get me whipped or worse…or they could take away my endos, lock me up where I can't get them, or—"

"We're going to get you out of here."

So casual, as if it happens all the time, just requires some dedication. When in fact nobody ever gets out. In Shael's whole life they haven't heard of such a thing. Sure, there are the legends of wild escapes in the early days of the camp. The corporation itself endorses those stories, they're among the licensed texts, children's tales where a cunning criminal finds a weakness in Flint's security and sneaks out. But, the camp's child-trainers explain, every loophole that the anti-heroes of such stories exploited has since been closed. The fences electrified. Surveillance units refined. Disciplinary protocols for guards who are discovered to be unfaithful to the corporation are much harsher now— as are the punishments for would-be escapees. Those children's stories always make clear that there's nothing worth encountering beyond Flint's supported life/work zone anyway. It's necessary for Flint to *support* its lucky participants because life and work elsewhere is *insupportable*. The participants of *Killer Kanta* or *The Old Sun*, say, escape the camp and discover only barrens, scarred earth and murderous heat, the soil still pregnant with radiation from old wars, causing horrific mutations in any escapee who tries to sustain themselves on fruit and vegetables: a second heart developing inside their chest until it bursts from their torso, for example. In such stories, the freedom seekers typically try, and fail, to stagger back to Flint's gleaming medical facilities in time to ease their pain and save their lives. The absence of drinkable water is another recurring theme: according to the stories, desiccated are the rivers and lakes, the streams and springs where an adventurer in earlier times might have refreshed themselves. The oceans persist, but far beyond reach, and so acidic as to be deadly to most of the creatures who once dwelled there, let alone of any practical use to a solitary human voyager. In the world as it is now, the stories suggest, a participant would have to be extremely foolish to want to escape the camp's sheltering embrace. And it's impossible besides.

"You shouldn't say those things to me. Please. You know there's no way out."

"Of course there is. There have always been successful escapes. You just don't hear about them. They get covered up as removals to correction centres, or in other ways. Even the families don't always know."

"So how do you?"

Coe stares at them levelly. "How do the items we make in here reach the mountains?"

"The transports."

"Right. Which always run smoothly. Because Flint guards are always so reliable. So committed to their work."

Shael raises an eyebrow.

"The camp is porous because of the transports," Coe goes on. "Before they reach the mountains, the transports often...leak. Food, information, tools—and *people*. There are no surveillance units out there."

"There's nothing at all. How do those people not die?"

"They have help. They're collected by our friends."

"How is that...where...?"

"Our friends in the Waste."

Shael inhales sharply. "There's nothing in the Waste. No one could survive there."

"It's been reclaimed."

"Impossible."

"Where did you learn that? Who taught you?"

"Everyone. Every text. Elders, trainers. No one's ever suggested—"

"They don't just lock up your body and break your will in here. They shackle your ability to imagine what else might exist."

Shael slides off the examination table, scoops their gown from the floor. They return it to their satchel and begin to put their regulation robe back on.

Coe doesn't move. "If I could help free you, would you go?"

"What kind of question is that? What you're describing isn't even—"

"If we could leave together. But probably you could never come back."

"And my kin?"

"Would stay here. For now. Until we grow stronger."

"*We.*"

"The settlement in the Waste. Which we'd join."

Shael shakes their head. "Everything you're proposing sounds..."

"I'm making this offer because I trust you. And because I don't want to be away from you."

Shael turns to face him. Coe places his hands on their hips, draws them close.

"But I need to know if this interests you," he continues. "Otherwise I won't mention it again. If you're not joining us, the less you know the better."

"What if it's just an elaborate form of suicide?"

"There are serious risks involved."

"They could retaliate against kin."

"Past escapes haven't led to that. Not open retaliation, at least. To make a public example of kin, the corporation would have to admit there's been an escape. They can't afford to admit that even once."

Shael stares at his lean shoulders, shining in the pale light. "I want to be where you are," they say. "But I don't understand…you say we'll get out, but get out and do what? Sicken and starve?"

Coe's eyes flash. "We get out, grow stronger together—and we fight back."

HEAT TIDES SHIMMER OVER THE CAMP BLOCK'S
centre court, crowded with dozens of giddy participants. Their Sanem-
laced laughter is macabre, a sludge of forced feeling. Or so Shael hears
it, through their own mandatory Sanem haze.

"Better to be sad than happy like this," they say to Coe.

It's late in the day, so cool enough to permit participants to occupy
the centre courts, exposed to the elements. At other times, condemned
participants are shackled in centre courts without cover until they
roast. Even in the coolest minutes of a celebration day such as today—a
pleasure conceded to the obedient—sweat swamps the revellers, glis-
tens on skin. Without Sanem, even these hours of calculated mercy
would be an ordeal.

Shael's kin are gathered by the court edge, where there's shade.
They eat savoury stew provided by the corporation, sweet pastries.
Everyone needs leisure, intoned the narrator of the film they were all
required to watch earlier in the day, its conclusion timed to coincide
with the Sanem activating in their bodies, a transition marked by
telltale giggles. *Flint assessors have dedicated years of research to iden-
tifying the elements necessary for a happy human life, and the proportion
between those elements. We provide the fullest range of satisfactions.* All
Flint "requests" in return are participants' labour and quiet. That they
should never demand more than the merely necessary. Never chal-

lenge the naturalized hierarchies—assessor, corrector, technician (medic, trainer), guard, participant—and the tacit hierarchies among participants themselves. In exchange for obedience: some festive time with friends and kin, once in a while. Even relatively unsupervised. Just pacified by Sanem, and the kind of laughter it elicits, not exactly convulsive but uncannily easy, liquid, smooth.

"If we want to play with the toys we make here, we have ten days," says Coe, drugged eyes mirthless.

"You trust your friend?" Maliez asks, meaning Guard 937. Older than Shael and Coe, tall and commanding, Maliez has been a member of the Blood Moon from the start, when it constituted itself out of the wreckage of another group that had led a failed insurrection. "How much do you have on him?"

"Enough. The bosses are becoming harsher with those like him. He knows it. And there are many other friends quietly supporting us, not just him."

Maliez shakes her head. "We'll need to move in a way that gives him cover. It has to be fully deniable for him."

Sweat-drenched, Shael glances around. There are many other clusters of participants in the centre court, laughing and talking. No reason that their own bunch should stand out, drawing special scrutiny from the guards roaming the perimeter in dark robes cut just a bit squarer than those worn by male participants, masculine no matter the wearer's gender. Yet Shael feels watched as ever. They can't shake the anxious suspicion that all members of the Blood Moon, along with any sympathizers, must be known to the corporation. That Flint documents every appearance in the camp of the Blood Moon's symbol, scratched into furniture, etched onto latrine walls: an almost-sphere, with three wavy lines extending from its convex side. That every time members of the Blood Moon gather, they bring the assessors' file on the group a little closer to completion—with ferocious repression soon to follow.

Such violence would fall hard on any Betweens in the group's orbit. Not only are Betweens disproportionately made scapegoats, but their existence itself comes to light mostly when one of them is made an example, dragged before their fellow participants in a spectacle of maiming punishment. Their existence is acknowledged only in the violent act of prohibiting it. Shael is alert enough to those dangers to feel that a group such as the Blood Moon should seldom or never meet. Its members and sympathizers shouldn't stand together in a centre court. It should be a tissue of whispers.

Yet they also can't deny their pleasure in seeing the others, spending time in the company of people who share basic intuitions about life in the camp. Affinity of values, community of instinct. When, say, Drekon, another survivor of the failed insurrection, remarks through his own narcotic mirth that celebration days are the most depressing of all the camp's compulsory activities—a common view among this group—Shael feels sane. Their kin would never admit as much, would instruct them to be grateful for whatever relief their overseers offer. Or when Maliez mutters about how every corrector gets at least a little hard or wet when fulfilling their solemn tasks, how correctors are all basically rapists given a free pass by the corporation, official rapists, empowered to violate in the name of order—Shael hears this and almost vibrates with adrenaline. Rage sparked by truth. It mobilizes them. It makes them less afraid.

"We just lie under the shipment until we're out? Seems too simple," Drekon says, his speech dangerously uncoded as usual, his voice like a scar, the typical Sanem looseness undetectable in it.

"The solution's not technological," Trin says. An acquaintance of Shael's from training, with bright eyes and a delicate frame, she always brings clarity to this group's conversations. And the weariness of someone twice her age. "They control the top end. We're safest when we keep it simple. Stealthy."

Coe squints in the sun. "I'm tired of living on that level. Everyone shrinking themselves to survive. Or being shrunk. What's the status of the dance now?"

At first, the action they call the dance was meant to destroy an empty correctors' station in the middle of the night. That would lead to intensified repression throughout the camp, further eroding the corporation's pretense of beneficence and radicalizing new layers of participants. Now the dance is also to be a diversion. Not simultaneous with the escapees' exit—any explosion, let alone one in a correctors' station, would trigger an immediate camp-wide lockdown—but erupting soon after they've passed beyond the camp's outer wall. The idea: to lock them *out*, strand the transport beyond the camp if for any reason (discovery of illicit cargo, say) its drivers should decide to turn around early.

"We have the materials," Drekon says. "Assembly is no problem. Our friends have sent us that knowledge also."

Friends in the Waste. Coe remains coy whenever Shael asks about them. They're on our side, Coe says. They're waiting for us. Where did they come from, Shael presses to know. How do they survive out there? Isn't the soil poisoned? They have help, Coe says.

"The main trouble," Drekon continues, "is setting it up. Somebody needs to go in for correction and make the drop."

"Not a problem," Coe says.

"But you can't be caught with it on you," Maliez says, "and you'll need to find an unobserved moment—"

"I'll take care of it. I've been in those stations enough times."

If Shael didn't know Coe, they'd never believe that a participant could calmly break away from the corridor queue next to a correctors' station, slide to the ground against a wall, withdraw from his satchel not the remotely controlled explosive device hidden inside it but instead a vial of Sanem, and proceed, in public, to get high. Or that, after being hauled into the station and left alone for the briefest moment while waiting to be whipped, this participant could retain the presence of mind to affix the device to the underside of the correction bench. But Shael does know Coe.

After evening meal, Shael finds their mother by herself in the dwelling hub's kitchen. Flint prefers its participants to eat in their semi-private quarters, associating with just their immediate neighbours; the common meal halls are used only when training or work placements make return to the hubs impractical. So Potenza spends much of her so-called free time here, preparing the rations the guards deliver, sometimes enlisting the help of Shael or their half-siblings. Now she's occupied with the washing-up. Silent at first, Shael joins her, begins to dry cutlery.

In little more than a whisper, Shael says: "If I were to leave this place..."

"Use other words."

As if she knows, immediately, what they intend. As if she's always known they wouldn't last in the camp. Would die or get out.

"If I...have an opportunity..."

"Then you must take it."

No hesitation, no surprise. Shael is astonished. "You don't worry about retaliation?"

Potenza keeps her eyes on the dishes. She glances towards her bedroom, where Tann, the brutal man with whom she was rematched, lies sleeping. "You're grown. The overseers know it. What am I to do if you roam past my wishes, beat you?"

Their overseers would expect that, in fact. Parents are commanded to do so without exception, no matter how old their offspring. To normalize such treatment, stitch its inevitability into every moment of camp life. It's how Potenza punished Shael when she caught them expressing their contradictions as a child—"borrowing" makeup from her room, for example, along with a feminine robe or two, more tapered than the masculine equivalents. Yet she also tapped her networks to procure endos for them when they told her they felt they'd die if they had to "grow into a man." That they'd *rather* die. She didn't punish them then. She looked at them with a love that was half pain and told them she was afraid their life would be more difficult than most—even here, in this place of near-impossible lives—but if she could make it easier, she would. And she made contact with one of the camp medics who, she said quietly, owed her a favour.

"But I also can't protect you," she continues now. "There are others who will?"

Shael nods. Their mother doesn't know about Coe, as far as they can tell. But they've long sensed she's aware that someone like Coe exists in Shael's life: a lover, a protector. A danger.

"Good. I'd never stop you. As I didn't stop your father."

The plate Shael is holding clatters into the sink.

Potenza keeps her face hidden behind her hair, thick like Shael's. "Or maybe that's not the right name for them," she says.

Shael blinks.

Potenza keeps scrubbing. "How do you think I recognized the signs in you so early?"

Shael stands frozen, holding their breath. Their father—their *other parent*—was a Between? And attempted an escape?

Unruffled, as if the conversation is perfectly ordinary, Potenza places dishes and utensils on the counter in front of her. "There's no way to be certain of what happened. Killed when trying to escape, the officials said. I believed it. It wouldn't have done me any good to disbelieve it."

Anger billows from Shael's gut. But, long habituated to discretion under stress, they keep their voice quiet. "You mean there's a chance they could still be alive? And you didn't tell me?"

They can hardly remember their other parent at all. Fell suddenly ill and died, they were told as a child, when it happened—or didn't happen. They were told their other parent was a gentle person, someone who did as they were instructed, bending to the will of the corporation until it broke them, or until they just broke. Shael has always accepted that story like they've accepted all the camp's ugliness: as a misfortune that couldn't be otherwise. Yet it was a lie. Shattered in an instant, as if they've never believed it, as if they've always known the truth: their other parent, of whom they lack even a clear mental image, was *like them*—and could still be out there, somewhere.

Potenza remains impassive under their anguished gaze. Stacks dishes. Continues to go through the motions of ordering her household. "I didn't tell you what I thought could only hurt you."

"That wasn't your decision to make." Their voice barely comes out.

"It was then. I'm sorry if I made the wrong one."

Shael can't bring themselves to reassure her. They do understand: she was trying to protect them. But they feel so incredibly angry.

"I had to keep you safe," Potenza goes on.

"Safe and alone. In the dark."

"I'm sorry."

"Who could blame you? We're mistakes, errors in nature, people like me and…" *My other parent.*

"Shael…"

But they're already halfway to their bedroom. They close the door behind them softly, meticulously.

Their bedroom, a space all to themselves. Rare luxury for an unmatched person. But their mother insisted, years ago. Housed her smaller children, her children with Tann, practically on top of each other in the second bedroom allocated for their offspring. *He's much too old to share a room with them still,* she argued, *he*-ing them as always in front of Tann, so Tann wouldn't beat them to death. *And he's not going to share a room with us. It's the best solution.* An undecorated room they'd enlivened with impossible fantasies. Of living openly as a Between. Living with Coe. Having the liberty to occupy their days with work more meaningful than body-warping manual labour on the starsugar cake lines, mass-fabricating delicacies they themselves might taste once a year, if at all. Or their new placement in motor assembly, barely more interesting. Or whatever more complex drudgery they might be retrained for next, if their participant approval score keeps improving. They stare at the grey walls of their private dream chamber and know, with a hardening clarity, that none of what they want will ever be possible here.

There's a rap at the door. They expect to see their mother when it slides open, but instead it's Mertia, their smallest sibling. Half-sibling.

"Are you sad?" she asks, playfully shifting all her weight to one of her legs, risking a topple.

They force a faint smile. "No more than usual."

"Tann's sleeping, but he was in a bad mood. Make sure you don't wake him."

"Of course."

"You were speaking loud, I was worried."

"It's okay. I'll be quiet now."

She blinks in acknowledgement, dashes forward, and throws her arms around them, then runs back out, leaving the door to the bedroom open.

Sounds from the kitchen drift towards them: a tap running, a clatter of dishes. Voices murmuring. A few minutes later, Shael sees their mother approaching.

"Leanya down the hall has died," she says, not crossing the room's threshold. If their last conversation has rattled her, she gives no sign. "Ceremony tomorrow night."

"Thank you," they say, sitting motionless on the edge of their bed.

She nods and withdraws.

Leanya wasn't that old. Shael wonders how she died. The latest safety incident during work hours, this month's participant dragged headfirst into a machine that everyone on the line had been shouting for years needed urgent repairs? Or maybe she was caught stealing from her workplace or a meal hall, extra rations for her family, and was corrected just a little too hard. *An accident*, every corrector involved would say. Correctors never suffer any repercussions for murders and maimings. They're from the mountains, after all. They and their kin make the rules—and the exceptions.

Whispers about Leanya's death coil through the motor assembly training hall the next day. Caught with a lover, Shael's bench-mate says. A high-trust participant class, comprising trainees whose approval scores are exceptional (Coe's not among them), still they aren't told what kind of device the motor belongs to. They may never be told, even if this becomes their long-haul work assignment. Their lot is to do, not to know. But they know very well that they'll be punished severely if they fit a single bolt wrong.

"They found her with another woman," says the bench-mate, a watery-eyed young man named Reev. "In the abandoned infirmary wing."

Shael's hands, wrapped around a motor mount, are suddenly sweaty. "Oh."

"Nothing good lasts in here," Reev says, whistling through the gaps in his front teeth. "They tease us with a spot like that. Unlocked door. Just so they can snatch it away."

They'll never meet Coe there again. Now the abandoned infirmary wing will sit deserted for years. Coe is aware of other, similar spaces, alternative meeting points—but so is Flint. And they'll always eventually crack down.

"She was there with another woman," Shael echoes.

"Yeah. Wish I could've seen it. Too late now. The one dead and the other can't walk. Good as dead on this block. I give her a year."

Shael isn't sure what exactly sparks their rage—that their bench-mate is so callous, or that the camp produces such callousness—but they have an almost irresistible urge to shove Reev as hard as they can. Instead they grind their teeth. "They weren't harming anyone."

A crude smile inches across Reev's face, but before he can speak and elicit a response from Shael that will almost certainly wreck their approval score, a trainer passes their bench and both trainees fall silent. Eyes down.

The leave-taking ceremony for Leanya is held after evening meal. In the common room of the dwelling hub her family shares with Shael's, nearly forty people gather—members of each family in the hub. They presence her in words. The body is long gone: ash, and not given to them to reclaim. Leanya's father speaks of her love of song. Her brothers reminisce about how she could outrun them as a child. The women of the dwelling hub have arranged sweets from their secret stockpiles on the windowless common room's small tables, bolted to the floor.

They speak little, though they're the ceremony's organizers, as usual, the ones who make sure it happens without delay and with all present. The expectation that the women will do this work always bothers Shael. But tonight Shael isn't just bothered. They're *livid*. As they've been, more than ever, since Coe raised the possibility that they might not need to exist in these killing corridors forever. No one at this ceremony has mentioned how Leanya died, why she was killed. And no one will. Her desires—their specificity, the beauty and dignity of their risks, in this place—will be erased. Won't even be hinted at, except maybe with pity or scorn. Because even at a gathering like this, technically in violation of Flint's rules, everyone acts like a model participant. Or, less charitably: like a guard. Normalizing the camp's gendered divisions of labour, its compulsory vanishing of unlicensable appetites. Accepting that rebellion is unthinkable, too costly. And always ready to quash dissent when it flares in others, lest it endanger all those around them.

Not everyone in the camp is like that, of course. As Shael scans the tired, lined faces in the ceremony's wide circle, they know there must be others present who harbour a spark or blaze of defiance and worry they're the only person in the room who does. And they might find each other. They might even love each other, for as long as they're allowed to. Until one lover ends up dead, the other maimed. Nobody held responsible. The camp grinding on, same as ever.

As the ceremony turns into socializing, a woman remains inconsolable. She weeps, almost motionless, by the common room infoscreen. A man rests his hand on her shoulder; Leanya's brothers bend towards her, murmuring. Leanya's mother, Shael sees as she turns. Most of what she says is inaudible, but they hear her say, plaintive: "She acted as if there were no...she could never accept...*she lived as if she were free.*"

Shaken, not in the mood to talk to anyone, Shael retreats. They scan the room as they go. Tann, their mother's match, is bent over the sweets, clearly taking more than his share. Shael's younger siblings are with their mother. Vinsan asks Potenza if he can call up a film on the infoscreen, one of the ancient narrative diversions that help to pass what little leisure time they have. Their mother, exhausted, snaps: "We don't all want to watch that now. People are mourning, what's wrong with you?" Unconvinced, Vinsan wanders off to join Tann in pillaging sweets. Tann slaps his son's back—playfully, but hard enough that the boy stumbles forward.

When Shael sees Coe next, several days later in the hub block meal hall, they don't hesitate. "Yes."

Coe's eyes stay on his soup. "Yes?"

Shael's smile is as thin as the broth. "We need to find a new private spot anyway. Might as well be…" They gesture vaguely away from themselves. *Anywhere that isn't here.*

If Coe has feelings about this, he lets none of them show. "Okay. You'll be told what you need to know, when it's time. Soon."

Shael squeezes Coe's thigh under the table. An unusual risk. But when will they next touch or be touched by him? "Thank you."

That afternoon, a young man is beaten in motor assembly training. Dozing at his bench, he's shaken awake and dragged across the room. He's stripped naked; a correction paddle is used. Angry crimson blotches spread as his screams fissure into gasping sobs. Designed to leave few traces, the plastic implement must be swung with horrible force to mark the skin like that. Shael watches as if from a great distance. As if they've always known the camp to be a temporary arrangement, for themselves and in general, always sowing the seeds of its own inevitable destruction. As if they're already gone.

DAYLIGHT

TO SUFFOCATE BENEATH A THOUSAND CHILDREN'S toys seems an undignified way to go. Shael tries to take shallow breaths to avoid shifting the layers of items on top of their body. Through the crush of boxes, a doll in each, they can see an edge of Maliez's foot. They can feel Coe's heat radiating, or at least they convince themselves they can. Fear and boredom fuse into a tense alertness. Outside, in the transport loading bay, there's a steady patter of footsteps, low voices. Shael closes their eyes, counts the spots of light that dance in their field of vision. They imagine the quality and quantity of light they'll glimpse when free of the camp, their access to the sun no longer rationed.

The vehicle rumbles to life. Shael feels its vibrations in their teeth. It idles. Longer than is typical? No way of knowing. Finally it creeps forward. A set of bay doors can be heard retracting. Within minutes, if all goes as planned, they'll have passed beyond the camp's outer wall. Four members of the Blood Moon—Coe, Maliez, Drekon, and Trin—plus Shael, fellow traveller, vulnerable Between whose lover has intervened on their behalf. A year's worth of endos in their satchel. Minimal other provisions: water, snacks. For most additional life needs, they're entrusting themselves to the people in the Waste. A gamble that, coolly considered, feels ludicrous. But so does resignation to life in the camp.

The whir of the transport is steady, betrays nothing of the terrain they're crossing. By now they might be past the camp's perimeter, or they might still be circling one of the ring roads that ripple to the camp's edge. The transport's storage hold, their hiding place, is windowless, admitting light only through tiny apertures high above them. The stowaways don't need to know where they are, per the plan. In this, too, they're dependent on their friends in the Waste, who will raid the transport at a predetermined point in its journey. An armed robbery. The guards won't be allowed to see what cargo is stolen, so they'll never know what cargo they've carried. All but one of the guards, anyway.

Coe doesn't keep Guard 937's secrets. So Shael is informed that, afterwards, 937 craves reassurance, wants his hair stroked, Coe's arms wrapped around him. Coe considers guards to be despicable people who, given preferential treatment in licensed matches, have no grounds to complain of loneliness. Yet Shael feels that loneliness is built into the guards' function, how they're dehumanized by their task of dehumanizing others. And how this is even truer of correctors. Shael considers them among the least fortunate of people, for all their official advantages. Coe hates when Shael talks this way. Every corrector belongs in the incinerator, he says. And when Shael sees correctors in action, they agree. But they also crave a world where the role of corrector doesn't exist in the first place.

Guard 937 has been manipulable because of his weakness, but his weakness also worries Shael. What if he loses his nerve when his superiors question him? What if he's lost his nerve already, sold them out? He's afraid of punishment, Coe stresses. For 937, it's become a straightforward calculation of risk. He's too far in. Betraying them at this point would get him killed.

Does Coe play with 937 the same intimate games he plays with Shael? Does Coe correct the guards? This is almost to ask whether Coe corrects the correctors, a still more transgressive question. But correctors can't be bought off with sex of any kind. Correctors aren't prisoners, first of all, they're Mountainers, which grants them complete impunity. And if they want more from a participant than the task of correction officially grants them, it's well-known that often they just take it. *Official rapists*, as Maliez says. What's existence like in the mountains, Shael has wondered, that a certain subset of those who dwell there can grow up to believe that tormenting others could be a desirable way to spend a life? Have they been tormented themselves, the young men and women—all correctors are officially gender-determinate—who volunteer for that task? Or were they sadists from the start?

The guards, at least, unlike the correctors, can sympathize with the prisoners because they're unfree themselves. It was imprudent of Flint to create such an identity of interests between guards and guarded: a miscalculation useful to the Blood Moon, as well as to unlicensed couples seeking gaps in surveillance. When Shael thinks of Guard 937, they imagine someone with a heart like their own, who feels much as they feel. So they wonder: will 937 miss Coe? Will Coe's other lovers?

"Why do you want to take me with you?" Shael asked him on their last night in the abandoned infirmary wing, before the corporation's jaws closed around that refuge. "Me in particular. Instead of the others you bring here, or kin." "Because you're most in danger," Coe said. Not a satisfying answer. "And because the point of leaving is to become more free. More than anyone else, you make me feel free here. I want to take with me the little freedom I already have." A better answer. Shael kissed Coe's neck to hide the tears that sprang up and startled them. Coe, with his habit of responding to any sentimentality with a compensating roughness, gripped Shael's bum almost hard enough to hurt. "When we're out," Coe said, "we'll have our own dwelling. We'll be together whenever we want. However we want. And because we won't have to worry about being caught, won't need to exhaust ourselves with ploys for meeting, we'll be free to turn our energy to other projects. Like freeing everyone else in here."

The transport rattles over gravel. Coe squeezes Shael's wrist. Patience. More than ever, their fate is now beyond their control. But others have attempted such an escape before and survived, Coe and the others have assured Shael. Hundreds of forerunners, now encamped in the Waste. And hundreds more will join them, grow the community of escapees, until Flint plugs the leak. Pity the last transport when that happens; Shael can only hope they aren't on it now. Yet soon more leaks will sprout, more guards compromised through pressure and persuasion, whom the members of the Blood Moon still in the camp will organize. Eventually the corporation will be unable to deny the escapes. Those who remain imprisoned will discover that exit is not only possible but happening all the time, a steady hum beneath the camp's propaganda insisting on its own inevitability. This discovery will remake their consciousness, establish freedom as more than just a hopeless dream. The Mountainers, for their part, will become more keenly aware that they're outnumbered by those they've oppressed. And will increasingly find this imbalance to be a source of concern.

Chills run through Shael at the thought of the corporation rolling out its weapons of war, long warehoused, against a settlement of escapees in the Waste. Drones already sometimes conduct raids, Coe has told Shael. Their friends have developed defensive tactics, but they remain vulnerable. A vulnerability accepted as a price of freedom. Shael has asked many times how their friends are supplied. They must have food out there? There are networks, Coe has said. You'll learn more when we arrive.

The transport screeches to a stop. Coe's grip on Shael's wrist tightens. A volley of voices. Footsteps, unhurried, crunch gravel just outside. An inspection point? They were told there would be several of those but only the guards' papers would be scrutinized, not the transport's hold. Yet now the hold's hatch swings open with a hiss of compressed air. A shock of heat, light, an overwhelming brilliance that can be felt and seen even beneath layers of doll boxes. Shael lies as motionless as possible. They barely breathe. Coe's fingers, damp, squeeze them so hard it hurts. "For the children," a deep, rumbly voice says—one of the transport guards, audible intermittently during much of the time they've been in the hold. The voice betrays a nervous hesitation that alarms Shael even more. "Playthings." The inspector grunts. That person, or someone, leans into the hold. The doll boxes above Shael shift, skitter. Shael is facing upwards, will be staring directly at whoever's inspecting the hold if the boxes continue to move. They bite their tongue to suppress the impulse to scream.

A box comes loose and several more cascade. Fierce sunlight. Shael grimaces, squints. Above them is the inspector, in a dark uniform like a corrector's, square shoulders on a robe that flows to the ankles. The inspector appears to be a middle-aged man, with pale eyes like stone.

At least Shael tried. At least they didn't perish in one of the camp's hard correction centres, tortured to death when their Betweenness inevitably became known. The inspector stares at Shael. Shael stares back. The look in the inspector's eyes is flat, inscrutable. The guard with whom the inspector spoke is out of view. Shael almost shakes their head, mouths a plea: *You didn't see us, we're not here.* But of course they know it's futile.

The inspector steps back. "On your way." The hold's hatch swings shut. Shael sucks air in desperate gulps. A trick, no doubt. The inspector must even now be telling the transport guards about their illicit cargo. The escapees will be driven to some lonely edge of the plains, where their friends in the Waste will never find them, and abandoned there. This certainty of imminent death persists as the transport hums awake, rolls forward. Abrupt, overwhelming, a sensation from hours earlier returns to Shael: of sitting in the transport hold with the others and remaining motionless as doll boxes rained over them, the image of a plastic hyper-feminine pale girl grinning from the surface of each box.

Shael waits until the vehicle has been in motion for a while again before they venture a whisper. "What was that?"

"I don't know," Coe whispers back.

"They looked right at me. Are they one of us?"

"It's possible. A lot of them have turned. But I don't know."

One of the others in the hold issues a sharp *Shhh.* Yes: they should stay silent, not abandon caution, in case the transport guards somehow haven't been alerted to their presence. In the stillness of this hope, Shael thinks, for the first time: *That wasn't the light of the camp.* No way of knowing for sure; intense light and heat exist in the camp as well.

But somehow they feel certain. What they saw, that brilliance flooding through the unsealed hatch, was the light of the plains.

A region once synonymous with fertility, now scorched and irradiated, deathly. The camp's monopoly on organizing vulnerable human life depends on the devastation of the land around it. Flint rules because it feeds. Because everyone knows the ruined earth, poisoned in the wars, is incapable of supporting any isolated adventurer's attempts to feed themselves. Feeding a population now requires industrial conditions under which edible synthetics can be formed—which Flint provides. The apparent impossibility of subsistence farming, foraging, or hunting leads to a stark choice for those without power: submit to unlimited domination or starve. Hence the urgency with which Shael has asked Coe how their friends in the Waste are provisioned. Coe's answer is always the same: they don't go hungry. Those already in the Waste are, in their rugged way, surviving. But the fewer details discussed in the camp, the better.

The transport rolls on. A murmur of guards' voices is audible, no different from before the checkpoint. Perhaps the inspector didn't report them. The possibility shakes Shael's intuitions about how authority flows through the camp. Has the camp long harboured a large minority of rebels? How many people under Flint's rule—participants and guards and even those higher up—are disloyal?

Something strikes the transport with a thunk. A squeal of metal follows. The vehicle zigzags, accelerates, skids to an abrupt halt. For a moment there's thick silence. Then a sound Shael has never heard before outside of films, but which they know corresponds to the items manufactured in the 4000-series block under the strictest supervision. The gunfire seems to meet no object. Maybe someone's firing into the air. There's a clatter as transport doors are unlatched, slammed. A burst of gunfire, and another, with a slightly different cadence, lighter, faster, issuing from nearer by. Coe's fingers round their wrist. Comforting familiarity of that firm grip. Again the hold's hatch hisses open. Again the fierce light, heat. No hope of avoiding detection now: hands sweep through the doll boxes, brush them every way. A guard's uniform.

More than one guard. Shael hides their face, as if by refusing to see they won't be seen. Ridiculous, childish. Coe's grip weakens and his hand slides away, Shael almost cries out, another report of gunfire, and its reply, Shael bites their cheek till they taste blood, they turn and look: a scuffle in the doorway of the hold. Someone reaching in, someone else reaching for the reacher, grappling with them. The others in the hold have abandoned their hiding places, are in various states of alert crouch, half-hidden, not hidden. The struggle unfolding in the doorway is hard to make out, the figures all backlit, but to Shael it looks like a single guard, one they don't recognize, is fighting a person who looks like nobody else they've ever seen: an elder, with dark brown skin, deep-set eyes, and white hair winding almost to the waist. A long gun is strapped over one of the stranger's shoulders. Their robe is tan, hooded, without the subtle elements of design that distinguish a robe as either masculine or feminine in the camp. Shael reads the stranger as a woman around their mother's age. But they can't linger on such thoughts, because at that moment hands seize them.

They scream. They're dragged towards the hold's hatch. Those grappling there—the guard, the elder—hesitate, turn to face Shael and the person forcing them forward. Shael's knees scrape along the floor, elbows bang against boxes. They struggle, but whoever's holding them is much stronger. They glimpse Maliez, standing, bracing herself against a wall of the hold, head craned forward under the low ceiling, eyes wide. It must take Shael no longer than a few seconds to reach the hold door, though it feels like minutes. The light overwhelms them. They squint. As they're about to fall onto the hard earth of the plains (it must be), a place they thought they'd never in their life encounter, a body slams into them, and into the person who's dragging them. They topple from the hold. A cloud of red-brown dust erupts around them as they collide, sprawling, with the ground. There's a short rattle of gunfire, extraordinarily loud. They scream. Their body hurts where it landed, but only there. Gunfire again. They cram their fingers into their ears, cough out the dust that chokes them. The sun is so hot. Consciousness flickers. But they fight the dark's seduction: if they pass out here, in this shadeless place, they feel certain they'll die. They keep their hands pressed over their ears as, again and again, call and response, gunfire rings out. They can see almost nothing through the dust, nothing but dark figures in frantic, ghostly motion.

They can't be sure how much time has passed when hands latch onto them again, strong but gentle. Like before, they can't be sure whose hands these are. But through the dust, they see now, steps away, the elder with the long white hair. The elder's face is, if not quite serene, entirely without violence. Their eyes meet. The elder smiles, or seems to; when Shael blinks, the smile is gone, and they wonder whether they imagined it. They feel themselves lifted, carried. This movement activates the ache in their body, everywhere, throbbing. They swallow a sob. The sun is monstrous, majestic. The sky cloudless: a hazy, blue-tinged grey. When they turn their head, the land all around them is an uninterrupted table of dirt and sand, pocked with ridges but flat enough that the horizon can be seen, shimmering, a long journey away. The plains. Shael shivers in the heat, sweat rolling down their neck. They fight to keep their eyes open. If they close their eyes, they'll pass out. Their vision swims. A cool hand, the elder's, strokes Shael's cheek. No one, not even their mother, has touched them like that since they were a child. Their eyes fall shut.

SURFACING

SHAEL DREAMS THE OCEAN IS CLEAN. SOMEHOW they recognize it as a dream even while they're in the midst of it. *I'm dreaming*, their dream self observes. But the observation fails to wake them. In the dream it's daytime, the sun high. They're with their mother and younger siblings, huddled beneath a fabric canopy that ripples in the breeze, all of them eating something delicious, of the earth, a plant. Observing the water from across the beach. The clean ocean. Tann, their mother's match who beats and berates them all, isn't there. With relief, Shael senses Tann is dead. They approach the waterwatcher on duty, who sits atop a short glass tower. We've tested it, the watcher says. We have never seen acidity this low in the centuries we've been testing it. We invite you to submerge yourself. Go ahead, begin with your toes. At your own risk, of course.

Preoccupied with eating, Potenza and the children hardly notice Shael's departure. Only young Mertia watches, wordless, as Shael drifts towards the ocean. The hot sand beneath their bare feet compels them to keep moving. They reach the water and it feels like water: impossible to tell if it is in fact, miraculously, clean. It rises around them, engulfs them. Keeping their eyes open, they walk for a minute under the waves, and the minute turns into an hour, the hour into days. The sand underfoot is cool. The water clear. They can see everything. Maybe this is what the waterwatcher on the beach meant by cleanliness: this clarity.

But what it reveals is that the ocean is empty. Without plant or animal life. Perhaps this vacancy, this evacuation of vitality, afflicts only the local region. Perhaps when they travel farther, they'll encounter the ocean's population. Its survivors. But wherever Shael walks, and even when they swim away from the ocean floor to investigate higher regions, there's nothing. Just them and the water. And a keen loneliness.

When they surface from the dream, its atmosphere seems at first to infuse the environment they've woken into, where it appears to be night. They ache everywhere. Naked apart from their underwear, a light sheet covering them, they lie stretched across a hard bed. They lift their head; their neck throbs and they release it. As their eyes adjust, they see they're inside some sort of tent. Its walls look seamless: no visible door or flap, no obvious point by which light might enter, though the darkness strikes Shael as too deep for daytime. They sense, without evidence, that the tent's walls would be translucent under the sunlight of the Waste. Strange how sure they feel that that's where they are.

"Don't try to move too fast," says an alto voice with the accent of the mountains: crisp, each word separated sharply from the next. A corrector's accent. "You need time to recover."

They turn towards the voice, just beside them. Its owner has long, straight bronze hair and soft, open features. A young woman around Shael's age, to judge by appearances. Most of the stranger's robe is dyed blue, shading into deep lavender in its bottom half. The colours are striking, if faded, perhaps from long exposure to the sun. The stranger's eyes are light, skin paler than Shael's. Paler than almost anyone Shael has ever seen—a fact that makes them feel a vague alarm, though they're too disoriented to fully process it.

"Where am I?" they ask. The obvious question, but their plainspokenness embarrasses them. They're afraid they'll somehow give themselves away as undeserving of survival, reveal that their rescuers saved a fool.

"You're where you were going." The stranger's eyes don't leave them.

"In the Waste," Shael says.

"Yes. Though we don't call it that. We call this place Riverwish."

A shiver runs through Shael, settling and tingling in their scalp. "Why?"

"You'd have to ask the founders. But many of us think with longing of the days when all the great rivers still flowed. When it was still possible in principle to live in equilibrium with the land."

Shael blinks. "I have so many questions."

"I did too, when I arrived."

"You came from the camp?"

"From the mountains."

They feel suddenly colder. "How is that possible?"

"More than possible, it's necessary. You think Riverwish could last without help from the mountains? This place survives on the goodwill and enterprise of traitors of all kinds. What would you like to be called, by the way? I know they called you Shael in there, but you can go by any name you'd like here. I'm Calla. She."

"Shael is...my name, that's...fine."

"You're the Between."

Their heart thuds. "How do you...?"

"We've been coordinating your arrival for a long time."

"So you...recognize...the way I...?"

A little shrug. "Of course. There are many like you here."

It feels staggering—both the fact itself and that she speaks of it openly. "And...in the mountains as well?"

"Oh, certainly. There's a kind of worship of iconic masculine and feminine physical forms there, the old archetypes we're all brainwashed to find natural, so complexity of your sort isn't exactly *encouraged*, but it's tolerated, at least when it's discreet. Not at all like in the camp. Where they'd kill you, yes? Or break you so harshly that you'd wish you were dead."

Shael just stares at her.

"It's so arbitrary," she goes on. "Cruel. Why should those parts of you threaten them? It makes almost no practical difference to them at all. Except for reproduction, in theory, but in practice they have all the bodies they need, even too many. There's no good reason why they can't just let you live. Except their *meanness*. As in *smallness*. They'll seize literally any opportunity to surveil and control."

Shael has seldom heard anyone speak so freely, with such confidence and frank scorn, besides Coe and the others in the Blood Moon—a defiance indulged at rare moments and great risk. This person from the mountains speaks as if such assurance is innate to her.

"Where's Coe?" Shael asks, startled to realize it wasn't their first question after waking. "The others I travelled with, are they here too?"

"You should rest now. Gather your strength."

They take a quick, shallow breath. "You won't tell me?"

"He was wounded. He's been returned to the camp, with another of your group, the one called Drekon. We believe they're safe."

A flash of panic hardens into dread. How can anyone on their side have made the conscious choice to send Coe back there? Don't they know what will happen to him?

"We control a whole transport bay in the camp," Calla says quickly. "All the guards on regular duty there are now ours. It gives us a latitude for action that would've been unthinkable even a couple of years ago. And several medics there are ours, with equipment we don't have here. We had to send your comrades back. I know it's hard to fathom, but I really do believe they'll be fine. By now Coe's wound will have been treated, the surveillance footage patched. I'm confident he's been reintegrated."

A whole transport bay. Within the camp's walls, but wrested from the corporation's control. *Ours.* It feels unreal.

"And the others I came out with? Maliez, Trin?"

"Maliez is here. Safe."

"And Trin?"

She averts her eyes, shakes her head. "I'm sorry."

Nausea churns through Shael. A hot wave of grief. They hadn't known Trin well; her poor health had often kept her from the training and work halls. Still, the news of her death is terrible. To spend half a life in the camp's infirmary, the other half a nightmare of pain and humiliation—trainers and correctors would never have much patience with frailty when it'd lead to slow work—only to be killed during an escape attempt. Intolerable horror.

And Coe absent. But safe, maybe. Because a transport bay in the camp is no longer *of* the camp. Astonished, drifting, Shael feels the weight of loss land on them for a moment—unbearable, it'll break them—and float off again. As sleep reclaims them, they wonder whether they'd have chosen to escape if they had known they'd be here without Coe.

They dream this time of midnight rainfall over the mountains. They've never seen the mountains, of course, but have encountered their sumptuous specifics in many unlicensed texts, penned by authors recognizable as Mountainers by their old-style names (*Sarah Johnson, David Mann*...)—so unlike the names in the camp, invented by the first generation of assessors and reproduced by parents ever after. Now, in the cacophonous torrent of the dream-storm, the parched plains seem briefly to darken, become for a moment again black soil, possibility. The air shimmers. Enormous steel spiders, at their centre a wide basin with a retractable top, crawl in columns down the mountainside. They inch across the earth, gathering their treasure of rainwater, beginning already, deep inside them, the process of purification. Soon the sun rises, and the spiders start their slow ascent back to the airlocked villas. The children of the mountains press their noses to the windows of their families' estates. Their delicate robes sway as the cleansed air, its quality and temperature assiduously maintained, circulates around them. The children watch the spiders climb steep rock slopes. They've never seen bio-spiders in their sealed houses, but these large machines—Explorers, they're called—are far more useful anyway, can be deployed not only to gather water but also, differently configured, to transport human travellers. And as weapons of war.

A dream of smashed surveillance beacons in the foothills of the mountains, sensors in pieces, coils and springs and hunks of steel lying scattered across the earth. Messages etched in sun-scorched blood on nearby rocks: threats of insurrection. *You will not know peace as long as you keep our kin in cages.* But no prisoner could have travelled to the foothills to write those words. Every Flint participant knows that such things are impossible. Every child pressed to their family villa's windows, gazing at the Explorers, knows it. No life exists or can exist in the vast region beyond the mountains and the camp, the dead zone, unbroken desolation till the start of Magent lands. How could it?

They surface from sleep to the sound of the Mountainer's solicitousness.

"I can leave you on your own for a while, or I can stay with you. Whatever suits you."

Groggy, they sit up, flinch at their full-body ache, dulled but still there.

"Oh, sorry," Calla says, "I thought you'd woken."

They glance at their surroundings: mostly unchanged, though the tent seems brighter now, its walls translucent, as Shael sensed they might be. "What is this place?"

Her robe's blue hood lies bunched around her shoulders. "We're in a tent in an infirmary."

"We're indoors?"

"Yes. This building used to house some of the town's central administration."

"Town."

"What do you think the Waste is?"

Vast desert, cold wind.

She pulls a metal tray from a grey plastic stand on wheels behind her, which Shael hadn't noticed. On the tray is a doughy nutrient roll and a cup of what looks like juice. "This is safe for you. It all comes from the camp."

Shael eats, drinks. A wave of nausea swells and settles. They don't feel great, but they've felt worse. They glance at the walls of the tent. "I was sure I was outside."

"Camped in the wilderness? That's how I imagined the Waste too." She nods towards the stand on wheels, where a folded robe and a pair of slippers sit next to a small white bottle. "Change into the robe, please, if you don't mind, and apply the cream to your uncovered skin. You may find the robe a bit warm, but it's more lightweight than it looks, designed to be breathable—the kind worn in the mountains when outside the airlock domes. Shields us from background radiation, to a degree. And it's important to protect your skin from the sun."

She leaves through a flap in the tent that's invisible until she presses it open. Alone, Shael dresses. The hooded robe is an even tan colour, not the patterned blue and lavender of hers. They wonder whether her robe's striking hues signify something about her role here.

The flap lifts and Calla returns with a masculine-appearing person, stocky and dark, in another tan robe. "This is Cuwam," she says. "Cuwam is a medic. He's been tending to you since you arrived."

"When was that?" Shael asks.

"You've been in and out of consciousness for a day, including the time it took to journey you here," Cuwam says. His speech bears the camp's accent, its subtle elisions. But his tone has a calm self-possession seldom heard within camp walls. "You took a bad fall, but you'll be okay. You must feel rather overwhelmed?"

Shael nods.

"I did too, when I arrived," Cuwam says. "It will pass. Calla is a good guide, she'll orient you."

"Thank you."

"It's nothing. You honour us by coming here. How do you feel?"

"Well enough," Shael says.

Cuwam nods, steps aside with Calla. They exchange soft words Shael can't make out. Soon the medic leaves and Calla returns to Shael's bedside. "I imagine you might like to see the place where you live now?"

They're more stable on their feet than they'd expected. In not much worse condition than after a poor night's sleep. Calla walks a step ahead of them, the lavender tail of her robe sweeping from side to side. As they reach the flap of the tent, she withdraws two pairs of dark-tinted glasses from a pocket of her robe, puts one on, and hands the other to Shael. "You'll want these. If not now, then definitely when we leave the building."

And indeed the room they step into, as they exit the tent, is flooded with light. Shael slides their glasses into place. They stand in a long, high-ceilinged hall, ringed by tall windows, lined with tents like the one in which Shael has been convalescing.

"Follow me," says Calla.

She leads them down an aisle between tents. Their slippers tap softly on the floor. Around them, stirrings: murmurs from the tents, flickers of robed motion at the margins of the room. They pass through stripes of intense light, cool relief of shadow. As they reach a door, another tan-robed figure appears in their path.

"A new arrival," Calla says to the stranger, who seems to be a woman maybe a decade older than they are, dark curls trailing from her hood.

"Yes, I'm aware. I volunteered to acclimate the other."

The other. "Maliez?" Shael asks.

"Yes."

Relief floods them. "May I see her?"

"She's sleeping now. Still recovering. We'll bring you together soon."

Calla frowns. Hesitates. "You've heard there's a raid coming?"

"We'll return to the west by nightfall, thank you."

"Mm. Yes." A tightening in Calla's voice. She seems uneasy, maybe even annoyed.

She guides Shael out the door, down a shadowy hallway with bare walls. Electric lights glow faintly, as if to conserve power.

"How long has this building been here?"

"A very long time," Calla says.

They descend a stairwell, their footfalls dull against the concrete.

"Does that person...not want me to see Maliez?" Shael asks. "Why can't I visit her now, even if she's unwell?"

"Because that isn't Abia's wish," Calla says, not looking at them. "And Abia does everything her own way." She tucks a dangling lock of bronze hair into her hood. "But you'll see your friend before long."

Through another door and they cross an airy lobby, the walls covered with graffiti, layers of it, a palimpsest. Mostly indecipherable, though there are several clear words and images: a scorpion, a bolt of lightning, the phrase *And the waters rose upon the earth*. A few more robed figures sit on benches. Sunlight streams through the building's front windows.

As soon as they step outside, Shael is aware of a sound they've seldom heard before: birdsong. "There's no sustenance for creatures near the camp," Calla says, a slight smile in her voice, when she sees Shael has gone still. "So they come here."

Whenever Shael has encountered non-human animals in stories, they've felt a shock of tenderness. Knowing what happened to them. The cascading extinctions. How they suffered.

Calla leads Shael away from the infirmary, down a paved, pitted road, in a silence broken by fitful birdsong. An iron gate stands open. Walking through it, they approach low grey buildings, glass facades on some, but many windowpanes missing. Alongside the intact buildings are ruins in varying states: exposed foundations, massive piles of rubble, structures that look whole for a couple of storeys before terminating abruptly in mid-air, deep cracks webbed through their walls. Layers of graffiti cover many surfaces.

"Did you paint all of this?" Shael gestures towards a set of markings: words in a language they can't read. "Your community?"

"No. The previous inhabitants. An age ago."

"Why? I mean, why take the time, when they were struggling to survive?"

Struggling to find food, after arable land and fishable seas were devastated, first by industry and the planetary heating it caused, then also by global war. Fighting to protect their territory from the heavily armed, amply provisioned newcomers who flooded the region, less irradiated and less fatally hot than areas to the south. At least this is what Shael has heard from elders in the camp. That was the period when radioactive waste was repurposed into weaponry, littering the planet with sacrifice zones. Caravans from the most scorched, bomb-cratered regions arrived here in vast columns, curling over plain and mountain like fat grey worms, digging in and warring to monopolize food, arms. Five leading caravans in particular, dominated by just twelve families, who built camps in which to intern captured rivals and anyone else who resisted or, facing starvation, simply surrendered to the marauders. Camps that consolidated into one enormous camp, a camp like a small city, a comprehensive life/work zone, in which the generations proliferated until no participant could remember anywhere else—besides whatever sparks of atavistic recall might be fanned by unlicensed pages of historians' texts.

"Probably they wrote on the walls for many reasons," Calla says. "To communicate with each other. To mark territory. To take revenge on those who'd owned the property. Or just because. Just boredom. Even in an emergency, it's hard to focus on bare survival. You don't survive if you do that."

Shael wonders how many emergencies she's lived through, this person from the mountains. "And what do you all focus on here? Besides survival?"

"Education, art. The administration of justice. Preparing food for the community, caring for the young and old. And fashioning objects we can use, such as bicycles. Several of these buildings serve as workshops. Many of us are also busy coordinating our relations with the mountains and the camp."

Shael's mind races. Before they can settle on a thought or question, a tall, broad person in dark sunglasses emerges from the front door of a nearby building, stretches with a yawn, and turns towards them. "To be with you here is a pleasure, Calla!" A deep voice. Warm.

"To be with you here is a pleasure, Natum," she replies, echoing almost exactly the inflection that the other gave the phrase. A customary greeting, maybe.

The stranger removes their hood to grin at them. Bald, handsome. "A newcomer?"

"Yes, this is Shael."

"You're very welcome," Natum says, scanning Shael from slippers to hood. "A big shock to arrive in this place, I know. Your new freedom! I remember that feeling."

"Natum here, he was one of the founders," Calla says.

"Calla will see to your needs well, but if I can serve you in any way, I'm yours."

"Thank you," Shael says, stirred by the intensity of the stranger's attention, the sincerity of his welcome. They're not used to being thought of, taken care of, by those who aren't kin or Coe.

"We provide for each other here. It's an adjustment, when all you've known is that hell. Everyone dominating everyone else just to survive."

That isn't precisely Shael's experience of the camp—they've seen as much co-operation as competition among its inhabitants, as much solidarity as rivalry. But they're touched nonetheless. "I'm grateful to be here."

"We'll see you again soon."

And with a small bow of his head in parting, Natum makes his way up the road.

Shael and Calla keep walking.

"How long have you been here?" Shael asks.

"Not all that long," Calla says. "Though I've adapted quickly. I'd been waiting to come here my whole life."

"You knew this place existed?"

"I knew it had to—or something of the sort. If it didn't exist, it would need to be built. The corporations couldn't be all there is. Human life has never operated like that. There have always been alternatives. In the margins."

The low buildings and ruins give way to a wide intersection. On its far side, two people roll by on bicycles. All around here, too, the forest has asserted itself, clambering over the road, which disappears entirely in places, walled off by plant life. The sky above them is a hazy blue.

"I love it," Shael whispers. "I can't believe it exists."

Eyes sparkling with amusement, Calla watches them. "I enjoy how everybody from the camp becomes a child again here at first. You're all so prematurely old. Even those with the sweetest of faces, like you."

They blink. "You're complimenting me."

"I suppose I am! Though it's not like you can take credit for your sweet face, exactly. It isn't as though they breed for that in the camp."

Shael wants to ask whether it's true that, as they've read, breeding in the mountains is far more deliberate: legend has it that the twelve old families mate only with each other. But they worry the question would be impertinent.

"Just the good luck of genetics," Calla goes on, playfully.

They can't be sure whether the fluttering in their belly is the result of this praise, what might be flirtation, or of the way it calls to mind their parent the Between who, maybe, escaped the camp. Where could their parent have gone, if they'd survived? "Are there other settlements like this one?"

"Not local to Flint's territory. Difficult to survive out here, as you can imagine. It's required a convergence of many factors to allow us to. Hard to replicate." She clambers over a tangle of branches, leads Shael along the edge of the road. "Supposedly there was a kindred settlement in Magent lands. But it was crushed a long time ago."

"Why hasn't this one been?"

"A broader basis of support within the camp, including guards. Important strategic allies in the mountains as well."

They pass down a narrow dirt road. For a moment the birdsong is all but deafening. Alongside this road, dense foliage gives way to wide, flat fields, land that might once have been used to grow edible crops, before the soil was poisoned.

"I didn't mean to be patronizing when I said you have a sweet face," Calla says.

Shael finds her tone unreadable. Maybe a little wry. Her face is appealing to them as well, though they wouldn't exactly call it sweet. There's a hardness to her eyes: not mean, but as if patiently set on vengeance. The lightness she performs is belied by something about her face, perhaps the cast of her mouth, that strikes them as enormously sad.

"I didn't mind," Shael says. "I'm like a child again here, as you say."

They drift down the road. "Imagine if we could safely grow our own food," Calla murmurs, surveying the fields. "The self-sufficiency that would be possible. How few compromises we'd need to make. It once was possible, of course. The land could support many people. Before we spoiled it."

Shael wonders whom she means by *we*. "You measure the radiation levels, then?"

"Yes. If you look closely at the birds and small creatures that feed on vegetation, you'll see they're often…not right. An extra eye, a missing ear, one wing or leg much bigger than normal."

"But they survive."

"Mostly. As do we. With the help of food from the camp. We raid shipments, or our friends there divert them for us."

Even if all the food Shael ever tasted in the camp was synthetic, manufactured in the carceral complex's vast laboratories, it's long been common knowledge among participants that Flint maintains fenced strips of farmland at the camp's far south end, near the mines, the soil tested regularly for radioactivity and subjected to experimental purification processes. Some participants are enrolled in studies where they're granted access to the bio-food grown in that area, their health tracked by assessors over a period of years. *Why do they even care if we're poisoned by contaminated food?* Shael once asked Coe. What difference would it make to the corporation if participants were to develop cancers over the course of decades? Yet Flint would never risk its prisoners beginning to suspect their autonomy might have a renewed material basis, might be possible for them as it had been for their ancestors. The corporation restricts access to bio-food not to preserve participants' health, but to constrain their hopes.

"We could farm here, in principle," Calla goes on. "There are comrades who attempt to grow fruits and vegetables. Lovely to look at, probably carcinogenic to eat—it's clear when we take readings of the soil.

But we'd risk it if we had to. We won't be starved out of this place." She shrugs. "Anyway, we have adequate supplies from the camp…most of the time. Those food transports are packed—one successful foray can feed us for a month. If the executives are going to satisfy their families' every want by exploiting captive labour, only fair that we take our share."

Shael observes her as they walk. "Do many people think like you do, in the mountains?"

"Hard to be sure. It's not as if it's safe to speak openly of rebellion there, though the penalties are gentler than in the camp. But there are others like me, yes. And reason to believe there are more in each new generation."

A small, dark animal flits across a field beside them. A blur of black fur. Shael stares.

"We're further in time from the emergencies that gave the camp a semblance of necessity. Or no, it never had that, but its propaganda was vaguely plausible, maybe, in the first generations. When the camp could still be seen as a temporary solution, a makeshift in an age of catastrophes, not many of my people would speak against it. But that time has passed. Every person born in the mountains today is born a tyrant, by default—a beneficiary of evil. So yes, today there are also more of us who refuse."

"You speak well," Shael says.

"I was raised to, I suppose."

A blush rises in them. A sudden pulse of shame. They feel it burn from their throat to their forehead. They were raised to be nothing. To work and suffer.

"You speak gracefully as well," she adds. "With a quiet boldness. You were always freer than many of the others in the camp, weren't you."

"As much as I was able to be," they murmur. They feel sweat gathering beneath their small, almost-deniable breasts, and they think: *As much as I had to be.*

"We'll turn here, I want to show you something."

Whispering leaves, hissing walls of green and brown. The forest's canopy blocks most of the sky, admits only pockets of light. The dirt road becomes more uneven, hilly. Birds screech. Shael glances up to see an explosion of movement—wings beating, branches jostled—then sudden stillness. After a few minutes' walk, they pass into a small clearing, at the centre of which is a low stone wall around a sprawling brick house. Unlike most of the built structures near the infirmary, this one looks perfectly preserved: windows intact, every brick in place.

"Does someone important live here?" Shael asks.

"You might say that."

They approach. The clearing is a patchwork of tall grasses that whisper as they sway, crunching beneath the visitors' feet. Past a stone well, a shed that Calla says serves as a latrine. The door of the brick house is unlocked; it swings open without a creak.

Shael feels a relief of cool air on their face as they step into the house. Only then do they realize how overheated they were becoming under the intense sunlight. Their slippers tap against a white-and-black tile floor with a slight shine, disturbing a silence that seems perfect—but only for a moment. From across the house, not far from them and somehow also very far: music. A piano. Shael recognizes the sound from films. There's music in the camp—on celebration days, in some work zones—but never live. No instruments. Never, like now, so nearby and at the same time so far away. They continue down the hall. The walls are bare, the corridor filled with the scent of fresh-cut flowers, though mild, not like the scents manufactured in the camp that mimic these. In its every detail, the house strikes Shael as *clean*.

The hallway opens into a wide, bright room. An assortment of soft chairs, occupied by robed people of many ages, sizes, shades. Through a bank of windows, sunshine and green. At the far end of the room: the piano. A tall person sits before it. The hood of their robe lowered, dark hair cascading in waves almost to the piano bench. Like the others in the room, Shael and Calla watch the pianist play. The music is sprightly, with an undercurrent of longing, perhaps a note of menace. At a pause, the pianist glances over their shoulder and meets Shael's gaze.

Only then does Shael observe the room's occupants more closely. Only then do they notice that many others in the room appear to be... like them. The elders are more immediately legible as such, Shael thinks; it's subtler among the youth. This thought is followed at once by another that knocks the air from their chest: *There are elders here.* Elders like them. Openly so, and surviving. Not purged, not disappeared into hard correction centres, not forced to deny, deny, deny. And the elders here sit alongside the young, without division, listening together to the music. A wiry, muscular youth rests their head against the full chest of an elder, whose long white hair casts the youth's face in shadow. Others sit together with more physical separation but still a palpable shared comfort. Maybe some are kin—though Shael also senses, in permutations difficult to parse, webs of desire curling through the room.

Motionless, Shael and Calla listen in silence until the pianist concludes. The others gathered notice the newcomers, steal glances at them, but mostly remain focused on the music. The end of the performance is greeted with quiet, attentive stillness from the listeners. With a nod, the pianist stands and leaves the piano, settles in a chair nearby. Calla drifts towards them, Shael following.

"May we join you?" she asks.

The pianist nods, brushing their hair from their face. They remind Shael of the elder glimpsed at moments in the blazing daylight of the plains, during their escape from the camp: waves of hair flowing nearly to their waist, deep-set eyes. They meet Shael's glance briefly, look away. A gesture of apprehension, Shael wonders, or a norm here, a convention of respect? It takes a moment for them to realize they habitually do the same.

"You've just arrived," the pianist says, not a question.

"Very recent," Calla answers for them.

"This house is a sanctuary," the pianist says. "For whoever needs it. But also for us. Those like us."

Shael struggles to find their voice, any voice. "All of you…"

"Most of us. Yes." The pianist's eyes trace the room. "We come here when we want to be among others like ourselves. But we aren't separate from the rest of Riverwish, not as a rule. The opposite. Your guide may have told you."

"I've told them little," Calla says. "I want them to adjust gradually."

"She's concerned you'll get the decompression sickness." A ghost of a smile plays at the pianist's mouth. "When the oceans were alive, people would make use of technologies that allowed them to descend to the depths. If they surfaced too quickly, they'd become ill. Sometimes they'd die. The same is true of people who come here from the camp. But less true of those like us. We tend to have more experience of freedom already when we arrive. In our fashion."

"That's right," Shael says. Calla had made a similar observation, but it feels different when another Between says it. Pride swells in them.

"You've been afraid for so long," the pianist says to Shael. Not a question. "And fear isn't absent here. There are raids. Nor is there always peace within Riverwish. But there are possibilities for pleasure and becoming here that probably you've never dared to dream of. And we can live them outside the walls of silence. As our ancestors did."

Ancestors. To Shael the word means others born in captivity. "Who?"

The pianist glances around the room. "Some of us are descended from the oppressors. Most of us, in some measure. Time mixes blood. But it isn't the oppressors' wisdom that guides us. Many among us retain a memory of older forms of knowledge. Our frameworks for justice, for example: elements of them can be traced to societies that were able to survive on the land for millennia. And in many of those societies, in those visions of justice, people like us were honoured. We were asked, and able, to counsel and heal. As we do here."

It strikes Shael abruptly. They turn to Calla. "Cuwam. The medic at the infirmary."

"Not quite like you, not a Between," she says. "But yes. A man by way of becoming."

In the camp they had no name for this kind of person, someone who lived fully as a man or woman despite having been assigned otherwise in the parturition hall. They had no name for this in the camp because in the camp it was impossible. Such would-be converts could not pass over, were rendered Betweens by default. But Shael knows that such people are their kin. Wayfarers on the same roads, whatever their destinations.

"When did he...he got access to endos here?"

"What you can get in the camp, we can get here," Calla says.

"You haven't lost anything by joining us," says the pianist. "I promise you."

Except their mother, their siblings. Coe. "People I care about are still trapped in that place."

"Temporarily. As I'm sure you've been told, our freedom here entails a responsibility to free those left behind. Riverwish would be an unconscionable project were that not true. Inconsistent with our ideals of justice. As long as one prisoner remains caged, we are not free. And not safe."

"A raid may be coming," Calla says.

"We know," says the pianist. "We've made preparations."

"Where did you learn to play?" Shael asks, their gaze lingering on the piano.

"I've been here a long time now. You'd be surprised what returns to you. What comes to you more easily than it should. Shades of ancestral memory."

And there is indeed something ghostly about the room, its occupants. The time they occupy is not the time of the camp, maybe not even the time of the rest of the settlement. Even the young ones give Shael this impression. In fact, the more Shael observes those around them, the harder it is for them to determine who's a youth and who's an elder.

"We'll leave you to your rest," says Calla. "Thanks for the music."

"Pleasure," says the pianist, eyes averted.

In the hallway, slippers clicking softly against tiles, Shael looks at the staircase that winds upwards in front of them. "Do they all sleep in this house?"

"Mostly they don't." Calla hesitates. "But there are bedrooms."

Shael glances over their shoulder, towards the room they've just left. "I'd never heard music like that."

"Bradoch is an angel," Calla replies. "Though they'd chide me for using such sentimental language."

Someone descends the staircase. The person appears to be a young man—and exhausted. Eyes downcast, bloodshot. Head heavy, gait slow. Startled, Shael gives Calla a questioning look. But she's already put her hood and sunglasses back on, and her pace is steady.

They emerge from the house into cacophonous birdsong. Fierce light, now slightly diminished. Their robes swish against the tall grass. As they begin to make their way back to the trail, there's a sound nearby: a human voice, neither speech nor song—a yawn. Shael turns and sees, around the side of the house, in a clearing within the clearing where the tall grass abates, a person bent double. Not in apparent distress; just stretching, maybe, or pausing for breath in the midst of a task. Around them is a tidy garden: radiant blooms of purple, scarlet. The first such flowers Shael has ever seen.

"Do you know them?"

"We all know each other," Calla says.

A slight frame that curves ambiguously; perhaps the stranger is a Between as well. They appear to be deep in thought, or anyway distracted. If they notice they have company, they give no sign. Sunlight glints off their dark glasses.

"Daekin spends much of their time here," Calla says. "That's their garden, really. Others tend to it, but the understanding is that it's Daekin's."

Shael's gaze is steady, their breathing slow. "Who are they?"

"Someone who always tells the truth, even when it's dangerous," she says. "So their life hasn't been easy."

"Why speak to me in code? Is there surveillance here?"

Her eyebrows lift. "Decompression sickness, remember? You're not immune. I want you to adjust at a safe pace." She smooths the bottom half of her robe, where its blue shades into lavender. "We make dyes from those flowers they tend. For our robes, among other things.

It's a simple way of resisting uniformity, no more than that. Certainly not a marker of any status distinctions."

"When did they arrive? Are they recent like me?"

"No, they were among the earliest here. You'd think that would be enough to secure them some reverence, or at least a little respect."

Daekin paces along the edge of the garden. They bend to observe their flowers.

"There isn't a lot of serious conflict in our community," Calla goes on, "and when it happens, our protocols are usually excellent. But when they fail..."

Her words hang in the stillness.

Shael doesn't know what to say. Their gaze lingers on the gardener.

"Thank you for showing me this place," they murmur. "I feel like I'm dreaming."

"Funny you say that. I've often thought that if I'd been born in the camp, I'd have convinced myself I was dreaming. I wouldn't have believed the camp could be reality. Such horror. But everyone who arrives here says it's Riverwish that feels like the dream." She takes their hand, squeezes it. "Shall we go on?"

A pulse of desire surges through Shael. Their body must have been handled in the infirmary, but they have no clear memory of anyone touching them since the transport, when Coe's palm slipped from theirs. The memory hurts. But they return the soft burst of pressure she's transmitted to their fingers, their palm, and together they walk on. The forest enfolds them as soon as they descend a few steps along the trail. When Shael turns to look behind them, they can no longer see the house.

Back the way they came, to the street of low buildings not far from the infirmary. Inside one building—unremarkable grey facade, rooftop of solar panels casting blinding reflections—a staircase winds down to an expansive basement cavern: the settlement's food hall, Calla explains. Rows of long wooden tables fill the room. A few people emerge from a doorway along the room's far wall, steaming plates in their hands.

Shael and Calla cross the room and enter a narrow chamber where food is laid out in trays, as in the camp's meal halls. Without formalities, no guards scrutinizing the size of their portions, they help themselves to a rich stew: a synthetic beef, rice, and vegetable mixture available in the camp only on some celebration days. Through an open door beyond the food trays, Shael can see people at work in a kitchen, tending pans on stoves, bent before a stone oven.

"Are they all men in there?" they wonder aloud, as they settle with Calla at a table. The hall is almost deserted apart from them, just a handful of others scattered in small groups.

"Men do most of the domestic work here," Calla says. "Women and those like you are typically in charge of deliberative processes, official leadership functions. The early arrivals made it a priority to overturn the gendered order of the camp. Resocialize everyone."

"Did it work?"

She hesitates. "I guess you can judge for yourself. A reshuffled order is still an order, with various difficulties. But you won't find many women staffing the food hall here."

The stew tastes better than anything Shael has tasted in a long time. "Women are the real leaders in the camp as well," they say, not quite finished chewing, hunger and excitement in competition. Heat rising to their cheeks, they cover their mouth. "Women organize dwelling hubs. Social relations between households. They get no credit for it, but everyone knows."

"But officially most authority is male there, yes?"

"Men act like they're in charge in the dwelling hubs. And a lot of the guards and trainers are men, though there are women among them. There are even some women correctors. Makes no difference...they always end up acting at least as viciously as the men."

"You'll never meet a guard or trainer or corrector again in your life. Only comrades."

Motion at another table catches Shael's eye. As a compact masculine-appearing person, grey hair cropped short, sits down, a group of feminine-appearing people nearby falls abruptly silent. They glance at the lone figure, who stares at their own plate with a strange intensity. As if with contained fury. After a moment, murmuring, the others rise and cross the hall, shooting glances behind them. A few climb the stairs and disappear from sight, while two settle at a different table. The solitary person sits very still.

"That's Caiben," Calla says, her voice low. "There have been some... problems with him lately."

"Problems?"

"I'd rather not speak of him here. Besides, you don't need to be plunged into all our complexities at once. You'll get to know them soon enough."

What evil must he have done, to be avoided like that by the others? What happens here when someone is dangerous to those around him, in this place without correctors or guards? Shael swallows the questions that swell in them.

After they've eaten, Calla brings them back to the infirmary, where Shael dozes awhile. They're woken by a low moan from nearby. Uneasy, they emerge from their tent. The day's light has faded and the infirmary hall's electric lights are dim, so they can just barely make out, across the hall, the source of the pained sound: a long figure draped across a stretcher, several medics crowded round.

"Another raid ambushed," says Calla, appearing beside Shael. "We sent a foray team to intercept a supply transport and secure rations. We were told all the guards in the transport had been turned, were friendly. They weren't. And they were waiting for us."

A memory of sprawling on the hot earth of the plains, amid a hail of gunfire, flashes through Shael. "I don't understand."

"We don't either. Our raids went smoothly for years." She smiles with unnatural abruptness. "A lot to take in! I don't want to overwhelm you. But there's a gathering you're invited to attend, if you're not too tired."

The meeting is held in an imposing stone building that Calla calls the council chamber. Once, she tells them, hundreds would gather here to worship invisible powers. This was in the days before Flint banned such practices, drove them underground, striving to erase them from memory as much as possible and constitute itself as the only law-giving authority. Now the building's interior is an open, unadorned space, with partially boarded-up window frames and a vaulted ceiling beneath which even soft speech swells with a faint echo. Occupied to near capacity: a majority of Riverwish's residents are at the meeting, Calla says. Several hundred people, Shael estimates. They assemble in a circle with a few concentric layers, everyone seated on simple wooden chairs.

"We name ourselves to begin, for the benefit of the newly arrived. Who's present?"

Shael recognizes the speaker: the long-haired elder from their escape, outside the transport, in the searing light and heat of the plains.

"Dorota serves as a leader in our community because she's widely trusted," Calla whispers to Shael, "but she has no formal precedence."

A tide of names eddies round. When it's Shael's turn, anxiety churns in them. Their voice barely comes out.

The meeting is conducted according to principles of non-hierarchy and direct democracy, Calla explains in a whisper. Elders' knowledge is treated with respect, but no one has official seniority over anyone else. If old enough to understand the proceedings, even the few children in attendance are entitled to speak and vote.

For the most part, everyone present contributes with humility and care. An elder suggests the communal kitchens are undersupplied; an attempt should be made to increase the amount of food siphoned from the camp.

"It would make the thefts more obvious. Too risky."

"We need to eat! It serves no one if we're weak."

"We knew that coming here would mean keeping our lives on a modest scale. We don't want to raise tensions with Flint right now. We're raided enough as it is."

Calla's mouth tightens. Glancing over their shoulder, Shael recognizes the last speaker as the same person who, in the infirmary hall, warned them about the coming raid. Who said she was tending to Maliez from the Blood Moon, Maliez who's here in the settlement, somewhere, but with whom they've still not been reunited. *Abia*—who insists that everything be done her own way, Calla said then, brittle. But now the speakers' list has moved on and Calla's face is again impassive.

"Much of the problem," says Dorota, "is that our supply forays keep failing. When we resolve that issue—"

"Because there's a spy!" a gravelly voice calls from the crowd.

"Our committee is working as quickly as possible. It helps no one to cast suspicions on our comrades. That's what Flint wants: to breed mistrust, fray our bonds of solidarity."

"They're killing us." The voice is soft and high-pitched. Another elder: a short, slight woman, to judge by appearances, seated across the circle from Shael. "They're picking off our strongest members on the forays that keep us fed. It isn't just psychological warfare, Dorota."

Shael recalls the wounded person on a stretcher in the infirmary hall. Low moans echoing.

"The committee understands the gravity of the situation," Dorota says. "We're drawing on all available information. Conducting interviews with comrades, especially those involved in any communication with the camp—and if we approach you for an interview, it does not mean you're under suspicion, I want to remind you all. Please give us a little more time."

There are murmurs around the chamber, but no one presses the issue further.

The meeting soon settles on one topic and stays there: the coming raid. Intelligence from the mountains suggests the incursion may be relatively small, a reprisal for the settlement's recent forays. Its goal is to destroy equipment in Riverwish, so weapons and vehicles not already brought underground should be secured immediately. They should expect the raid sometime in the next three days, possibly as soon as that same evening.

This report is delivered by a thin masculine-appearing person, as pale as Calla. "They want to give us a little *correction*. Little dose of the...what do they call them? *Correction paddles.* But we're used to that, aren't we. We're not fazed."

Almost inaudibly, Calla snorts. "Hans has never seen that sort of device in his life," she whispers to them. "He's pure mountain."

"I think we should limit our provocations," says the soft-spoken elder who spoke moments earlier. "It's not just the supply runs. Those are necessary. But the side trips into the foothills, to damage the mountains' rail corridor? Or the threats our militants carve into the side of camp transports? These serve no purpose. And clearly they provoke retribution."

Murmurs ebb through the room. They seem mostly to be assenting.

"With respect, I don't think it's right to lay so much blame on militants letting off steam." A deep voice, across the circle from Shael. Natum, who gave them a gallant welcome when they met on the road. "Discipline is important, but so is keeping alive a flame of rage against our torturers. I have no interest in staying huddled here for another generation. The goal is still to build our confidence and our strength to the point where we can take the camp."

Shael experiences such open talk of insurrection as a physical shock to the body. In the camp it would mean certain death. Equal parts uneasy and mesmerized, they stare at Natum.

"I don't think there's any danger that we'll lose our hatred of the camp," says the elder. "But I hear you."

"These are all important considerations," says Dorota. "For now, though, our priority must be to keep everyone safe from the raid."

"Anyone who wants to shelter with us in the west is welcome," says Abia. "Equipment we want to protect can be moved into the ravine."

"Thank you," says Dorota.

"We have adequate underground storage near here," says Calla.

"Safer in the west during raids," says Abia. "We know this."

Calla exhales audibly.

"How are our defence supplies?" Dorota asks.

"Could be better," says Natum. "I need a few parts to finish a propulsive mechanism. They've been hard to source. But once I get them, we should be able to blow their drones out of the sky again. I'm tired of scampering."

An approving hum runs through the gathering. A few scattered cheers.

"Working on it," says Hans. "Weaponry isn't easy to smuggle."

"No rush, brother," says Natum. "When you can."

"I do like blowing drones out of the sky," Hans says. "Makes a pleasant music."

Perhaps it's this jocular, outwardly uncomplicated masculinity that calls Shael's attention to the apparent absence of other Betweens among the meeting's speakers. They scan the room and spot a few of those they noticed at the brick house earlier in the day, Bradoch the pianist among them. But no Daekin.

When the meeting concludes, everyone issues from the stone building in one wave. They disperse swiftly—in case the raiders should take advantage of finding them all gathered together, exposed on the street. But for a moment, buoyed by the current of hundreds of comrades, warmed by their laughter and bold talk, Shael feels a thrill of ecstasy. More than they ever did in the camp, even on the fringes of the Blood Moon, they feel they're part of a movement, spirits united in a life-giving project. They feel like they're home.

A CLAMOUR LIKE THUNDER. HANDS ON SHAEL'S arms, shaking them.

"Wake up, we need to go. Now."

Shael stirs. The tent takes shape in the darkness around them. Calla's face, furrowed with urgency. Blasts echo, not far away; the building responds with a low rattle. Groggy, still in their robe, Shael clambers from bed. Moving decisively, Calla grabs their hand and pulls them from the tent. The infirmary hall is almost deserted. Those who remain are in a commotion, scrambling. Calla leads Shael past them, out of the hall, out of the building.

Wind incites the forest to a steady hiss, leaves whispering. The explosions are intermittent, flares that illuminate the night. Shael senses it's close to dawn, though it's impossible to be sure. Calla turns away from the road that earlier they went out by, guides them around the side of the infirmary, through mud and trees, to a low, wide concrete structure with a nondescript door.

Inside, pale lights flicker. The chamber is big and stark, its corridors broad enough to be roads: ramps, which appear to descend to lower floors. Calla tugs at Shael's hand, urges them on. Many others are taking refuge here. There are even a few infants, one of whom squalls as several adults try to quiet it. *They freed babies from the camp*, Shael thinks with a jolt of wonder—a sensation that only deepens as they realize the infants more likely began life here. Born into this dangerous freedom.

The population increases as they move deeper into the underground cavern. Shael recognizes faces from the meeting they attended in the council chamber. They pause at a floor where the pale lights illuminate at least twenty or thirty people in the shadows. Most of them look calm. They speak softly; some hold each other. The corridor seems to keep descending, but Calla leads Shael off the ramp. Gripping their hand, she guides them to a corner, where they both sit on the cool concrete. The shadows afford some privacy, though their nearest neighbours, a group of three people who appear to be young men, aren't far away. It takes a moment for Shael to notice how those people are touching each other. A hand cupped on the back of a neck. Fingers drawn casually along an inner thigh. Discreet, but not hidden. It's jarring to see erotic touch amid the hush and fear of those sheltering here, though it also makes a kind of sense. Sensuality as comfort. A reaction to, and against, mortal dangers.

"Desire is unashamed in the settlement, at least a lot of the time," Calla says, following Shael's gaze. "Do you find it strange?"

Shael hesitates. "Not strange, but…"

"We're told to be unashamed in the mountains, too. *Fulfill our perfection* through the pursuit of pleasure, girls as much as boys. But old and boring notions of beauty are worshipped, abstention is considered perverse, and so on. People from the great families think they're entitled to everyone's bodies. It's all pressure and presumption and lies."

Too much of Shael is still asleep for them to keep up with the pace of her thoughts. There's a distant rumble; subtle vibrations rattle them. How often is the community forced to hide underground like this, Shael wonders, and for how long must they all stay in hiding at such times? Less pressing but more perplexing: how could Calla have chosen this life?

"You could've just stayed where you were born and been comfortable. Safe. But you came here, to this."

Her gaze wanders over the others nearby. Couples, elders, many of whom look frail, perhaps malnourished. "We were told the camp was a kindness," she says. "A support for imperfectible people. Unfortunates. But I'll never forget the night there was a revolt in the camp and my father came home in a rage. I was small, already in bed, but I could hear him shouting. People in the camp had breached the perimeter wall. Stolen weapons from guards. Many escapees were still unaccounted for."

Shael is around her age, as far as they can tell: all of this happened while they slept in their own hard bed in the camp. What if their parent had been among those escapees?

A peal of laughter echoes through the underground cavern. The sound seems bizarre to Shael, given the circumstances. But no stranger than the conversation they're having. What do people say to each other when hiding from a sky full of death? They talk about anything but what's happening, maybe. The laughter bursts forth again. A child's. Yet no laughing child is visible. The sound seems to come from everywhere and nowhere.

"The next morning, at first meal, I asked my father whether there might be perfectible children in the camp," Calla goes on. "Would they just be trapped there forever, because they happened to have been born there? He was used to me asking all kinds of questions, but this one seemed to bother him. He told me our families had always adopted perfectible children from the camp when they'd come to sight, but it was extremely rare. Most of the camp's children simply aren't from perfectible lines, he said. The breeding assessors had made sure of that."

Her tone is casual. But her eyes flash with a rage that Shael recognizes—that they've seen in Flint participants their whole life. Could it be true, this suggestion that some children are spirited away from the camp to the mountains? *Perfectible children?* The sudden death of a participant child has never been rare and wouldn't be hard for Flint to fake. Vanishings in the infirmary. But if such things happen—and Calla's father could well have been lying—participants are given no sign. Ascendence to the mountains on the basis of "perfection," or for any reason, is never held out as a possibility. If it happens, it happens not to give participants hope that they or their children might escape their desperate circumstances, but to serve the Mountainers' obscure wishes. A chill runs through Shael at the thought.

"There's a magnificent library where I come from," Calla continues. "It's built on the highest layer of the inhabited area, an imposing tower. On the top level is an observatory deck, all glass and plush chairs and dark panelling, very beautiful, peaceful. I would spend hours there reading our histories. Young people in the mountains are granted maximum freedom to pursue their perfection, so I was able to access even texts that, it could be argued, are subversive of Flint's foundations. Histories that show the corporation to be no more than banditry made presentable. Brutal warlord dominion made respectable."

As if on cue, an explosion above ground rocks the cavern. Louder than most of the previous blasts. Closer?

"Sorry, I'm talking too much," Calla says. "We do love to rehearse our own mythologies."

We as in people? Or as in Mountainers, proud and buoyed by the stories they tell about why they're naturally superior to others? Either way, her embarrassment seems genuine; she flushes.

In the silence that falls, Shael's attention is drawn again to the three young masculine-appearing people nearby, now even more open in their caresses. Hands stroking hair, fingers drawing circles on a slender chest.

"You and Coe…" Calla says, watching Shael watch the others.

Shael's heart pounds at the mention of Coe's name.

"We were briefed about you," Calla goes on. "I'm moved by how you formed a match like that under the camp's conditions. Were you afraid?"

Always. "It was dangerous for us, yes. We were both officially considered to be men. Not the kind of match that's eligible for a licence."

"But you managed."

"The rules are inconsistently enforced."

She laughs. "Of course."

"They just want you to be terrified. To know that at any moment they might crack down. That any freedom you have, they can revoke."

She hesitates, her eyes on them. "You can be with any adult you want here, if there's mutual interest. We have a system, maybe you've noticed the signs. On the left elbows of our robes, have you seen?" She lifts hers. Sewn onto the robe is a discreet green patch. "Simple signals," she says. "Orange means the wearer is seeking no one—they're attached to one person only, or they're without sexual desire, at that time or in general. Red expresses desire for masculine partners; blue means desire for feminine partners. Purple means desire for androgynous partners. There are other colours and patterns that express more particular interests. And colours can be combined, of course."

Shael's smile is tentative. "You all put some thought into this."

"It might seem frivolous. But so much conflict stems from poor management of desire. Failures to organize desire, socialize it. And we don't have many sophisticated pleasures here, as you might have noticed. So we dedicate a lot of care to the pleasures that are available."

Shael hovers their hand above the left elbow of her robe, not quite touching it. "And this colour? What does it mean?"

"It means I like...anyone."

"Without preference?"

"I have preferences among individuals."

Shael points to the green patch. "May I touch?"

"Of course," she says, "it's just a piece of fabric."

As Shael moves their hand towards the patch, their fingers brush against hers. Their eyes meet hers.

"We could rest a little," she says, after a moment. "It'll be daybreak before long."

They nod. She stretches out on the floor, bunching her robe's hood into a makeshift pillow. She seems to be more or less at ease, despite the intermittent jolts and rumbles that the cavern's concrete transmits to their bodies. Shael mirrors her but struggles to get comfortable, squirms in place.

"You can place your head on me, if that would be better for you," she says.

They shift towards her, let her draw their head and neck onto a softness, mostly her arm though also her chest. She curls her other arm around them. They press closer to her. They almost even feel safe.

When Shael wakes, there's no way to be certain it's after sunrise. But somehow they sense it is. Around the cavern there's a stirring, others emerging from sleep. Shael keeps still, reluctant to disturb Calla. One of her hands is splayed in their curls. They wonder again how often such states of emergency arise here, how frequently this cavern is occupied. These thoughts are soon displaced by the immediate needs of their body: they've had nothing to eat since the previous evening before the meeting in the council chamber, and they need to pee.

In a small room at the centre of the cavern, a row of portable water tanks are separated from each other by thin partitions. As Shael emerges from this room, they almost collide with someone. Thick dark hair, serious demeanour. The person in whose company Calla seems always to grow tense. Abia.

"I was also in the camp," she says. "I know how startling this all must feel."

"It's...different, yes."

Would Calla be bothered by their talking with this person? Shael scans the room. Calla is around the corner, out of sight. No one seems to be watching them.

"She means well," Abia says, as if guessing the direction of their thoughts. "But it's worth remembering that she's from the mountains. Most of us aren't."

Shael hesitates. Doesn't know what to say.

"She can go home," Abia continues. "At the very worst, they'd put her in the camp. Even that's unlikely, given who her father is. The

Mountainers like to play saviour, it settles their conscience, but they don't always grasp what we risk. If we're caught, a quick death is the best we can hope for. Do you see?"

"I..."

"They love their pleasures and their processes, the mountain people. But both can be traps."

They wonder what she means by *processes*.

"Ask for me if you ever want to talk. Others will connect us."

Calla has stirred by the time Shael returns to her. The paleness of her skin is even more conspicuous to them than it had been. Surreal to be casually sharing space with a person from the mountains. A person from a family in possession of incredible wealth, her symmetrical features engraved by generations of ruthless breeding. The corporation's breeding protocols are just as calculated in the camp, to be sure. Flint's assessors have deliberately mixed bloodlines there, to blur any surviving ancestral distinctions in favour of the camp's own hierarchies. Never a fully successful project. Privileges still tend to accrue to pallor in the camp (*more of the mountains in them*): less horrendous work placements, a greater likelihood of selection for guard duty. Those who are darkest-skinned are targeted disproportionately by the camp's official and unofficial brutalities, often denied a high participant approval score even when their conduct is twice as careful as their paler peers'. Yet these dynamics are made ambiguous by the fact that all participants and guards look far more like each other than like Mountainers. No one in the camp looks like Calla. No one, that is, except the correctors.

Shael and Calla join a trail of people flowing from the cavern by the winding ramp. The sunlight is intense when they emerge, the sky a hazy blue. At first there's no sign of the previous night's raid. Only when they reach the front lawn of the infirmary do they see the building has been damaged. A section of its second-storey wall is missing, a heap of debris on the ground below it.

"Not the worst they've done," Calla murmurs.

Branches snap as others who'd been hiding underground tramp past them down the path.

"They send drones first just for surveillance," she says. "To try to map where we are. We don't make it easy for them, but they get an idea. Then the drones come back."

To live in constant fear of deadly raids. Intolerable. And still preferable to the terror of the camp, Shael thinks. There the threat of violence is stitched into every word and act, colours the corridors, shapes even the care exchanged in families. Here, from what they've seen, violence is mostly a threat from beyond, looming but external. Here the internal norm seems to be peace.

"I'm starving," Calla says. "Let's get food."

She leads them away from the infirmary, along the road, towards the squat building in whose basement is the food hall where they took their meal the previous day. The hall is crowded, dozens of comrades waiting in line to serve themselves or seated at the room's long tables. The swish of robes blends with a hubbub of post-raid talk. Plates filled, Shael and Calla join a table occupied by a group of men Calla knows well, she says. They're greeted warmly as they sit, but it's clear at once that something is off. The men speak with each other in a hush that's taut with concern. Their voices bear the accent of the camp.

"He broke a bone?"

"They think so."

"A rib."

"That's the worry, but we'll see. We have to wait for the scanner."

"And if he can't wait?"

"What can we do, we don't have the resources—"

"I always thought Caiben was a rat."

"He has a temper. I don't think he's a bad man, but in our situation, in these circumstances—"

"They never should have brought him out. Some people belong inside."

"I wouldn't go so far as that."

"If you can't live in peace with others, stay inside. That's what I say."

Shael glances between them, struggling to understand what's happened.

Calla just listens, eats her stew. Eventually, when a silence falls, she clears her throat. "Will there be a trial?"

Bearded, not young, with leathery skin suggesting long acquaintance with the sun—early arrivals to Riverwish, maybe—the men look at her as if remembering abruptly that she and Shael are there.

"As soon as it's clear that Natum's condition is stable."

Natum. A ripple of alarm passes through Shael as they remember the person who greeted them warmly on the street, made them feel welcome. Now injured by someone the community knew to be a danger. Even here, the long shadow of predictable aggression.

"The conflict was with Natum?" Calla raises an eyebrow. "I wouldn't rush to assume Caiben was the only one at fault."

"There were many witnesses."

"They're both too volatile," Calla says, a bit peremptorily, as if accustomed to having the last word. "I know the selections of comrades early on were…less discriminating, but we really must do a better job of second education. Especially for the men. I don't blame them, there's nothing biological or inevitable about it, but the camp turns them into such terrors."

And what does life in the mountains turn people into? Shael wonders, thinking of the camp's correctors.

The men at the table exchange glances, but their posture towards Calla is deferential. "There'll be discussion of this at the trial, I'm sure."

"Yes, I'm sure."

A strained silence falls. One of the men laughs awkwardly. "Sometimes I wish we had Sanem here, if you know what I mean. Take the edge off."

Shael recalls the false laughter of Sanem-drugged participants on celebration days, a sound they've heard all their life. Addicts showing up high to their work placements, getting dragged out. Disappearing.

"We decided against bringing Sanem here for a reason," Calla says, with a moral assurance that makes Shael at least as uneasy as the man's nostalgia for the drug.

"Who's *we*," the man mumbles. Then, quickly, another awkward laugh. He gives a little wave, a gesture of dismissal—*never mind, just kidding*—and concentrates on his food.

Calla eats in a hurry. Shael watches her, tries to keep up. When they've finished, she leads them to deposit their dishes in the collection area and mutters: "Bear with me, I want to find someone." Her gaze sweeps over the food hall. In a moment she gestures at Shael to follow her and leads them to a far corner, where a pale masculine-appearing person is huddled over a plate: the person who delivered intelligence from the mountains at the previous night's meeting. He shares a table with several others but sits apart from them, doesn't appear to be involved in their conversation.

"Hans," Calla says as they approach. Hans looks up, startled. Relaxes when he sees it's her. "This is Shael. They're new."

"You've joined our little family," says Hans, with a mirthless grin.

"You heard about Caiben and Natum."

"Of course. Can't say I'm surprised. I'll go out to meet a transport bringing supplies later today. Luckily we'd planned the delivery already, when we got word of the raid."

"Hans is in charge of coordinating the flow of supplies between Riverwish and the mountains, Riverwish and the camp."

"I wouldn't say I'm in charge, technically none of us are." Again that grin: brief, nervous, ironic. "But I help. I know the systems."

"Hans managed distribution for Flint. He was one of the most highly placed executives to join us."

He stabs at his food. "You're making me blush."

"I've never seen my father so furious as the day Hans left. It was illuminating, really. I also wanted to make my father that angry. And here was a proven way to do it."

"She flatters me. I'm nobody, just a humble servant of my comrades, one who happens to know a few things. The real heroes are those who stay in the mountains or the camp and stand with us in secret. Who supply us with food, materials. Intelligence. We'd be lost without their support."

Shael pictures Coe. Back in the camp, keeping a low profile, quietly organizing his friends, then prisoners who are maybe one degree removed from his friends but whom his friends trust, and at the same time testing the loyalties of the guards, seeing which can be turned, which can be bribed, which can at least be neutralized as threats. Without that type of work as a foundation, Shael could never have escaped, and any plans to liberate the camp would be pure fantasy. Gratitude mixes with longing for him as they think of it.

"We hear Natum may have broken a rib."

"Yes, right, we're securing a scanner and other surgical necessities. Thank goodness for Martina."

"And the trial?"

"Probably tomorrow or the day after, once more information has been gathered."

"Justice moves quickly but carefully here," Calla says to Shael.

"Depends who you ask," Hans says.

"You're cynical," Calla says.

Hans's grin flickers. "Ask Daekin."

Shael sits with Calla on a balcony that overlooks a mess of rubble that may once have been a house. Beyond those ruins, a dirt road winds up a hill, disappearing into the trees. This unit with the balcony is her current sleeping place, in a low, dilapidated building with hallways full of doors numbered like the camp's dwelling hubs. These aren't her permanent quarters, she's explained. Like most people here, she stays in motion, circulating from shelter to shelter, so the corporation's surveillance data remain always outdated, the accuracy and thus the lethality of a raid always in doubt. Must get tiring, Shael thinks. Never relaxing into a home.

Hearing how she wanders, they feel how little they grasp the map of this place: the extent of Riverwish itself, but also its spatial relationship to the camp and the mountains, and the shape of the world beyond that. How far is it to Magent lands? What other communities, if any, might exist between there and here? Where does the land end and the ocean begin? In the camp they were denied any clear understanding of such things. If the ocean were invoked there, it was only as *the unreachable, the impossible.* But now that Shael has left the camp, they want to know where the unreachable is located, precisely, and how it may be reached. The coordinates of the impossible, and how to get there.

Someone passes below the balcony. Shael is unaccountably certain it's Daekin: the gardener, the truth-teller whose life hasn't been easy. The passerby comes into sight: a thin youth with shoulder-length hair, not Daekin.

"What did that person in the food hall mean when he spoke of the one we saw in the garden?" Shael asks.

"You shouldn't take Hans too seriously," Calla says, gazing out over the ruins.

"But why did he speak like that?"

"Daekin was a critic of the community's earliest arrangements."

She doesn't immediately say more. Shael watches her.

"I don't know all the details," she goes on. "It was before I arrived. But it's said that when Daekin criticized matters, we were led, informally, by powerful men. In those days, the men in the unofficial leadership would…take sexual liberties. And they'd simultaneously position themselves as protectors of women—accusing their rivals of predation, sometimes scapegoating Betweens. It's easy to detect a residue of that time in a certain wariness of men that still exists in Riverwish. Not always completely fair to the men, in my opinion, but you can understand the caution. Anyway, Daekin saw all those dynamics, they saw how the real state of things was obscured by a rhetoric of sexual equality and freedom, and they spoke out. It didn't go well for them."

"But they were right."

"Of course they were right. But they were impolitic. They pointed at irresponsible power and were completely unprepared when that same power closed ranks to defend itself. It couldn't have been more predictable."

To someone from the mountains, maybe. The caustic thought surprises Shael. "Daekin is from the camp?"

She hesitates for just a moment. "Yes."

They feel a curiosity that almost becomes a question. But doesn't. Not quite. Not yet. Everything here is so new to them. They mustn't let themselves get the decompression sickness.

Watching her, they find her expression hard to read. The green patch sewn onto her robe's left elbow catches their eye. Idly, languidly, they reach towards it, place a thumb atop it.

"You're open to desiring anyone, but you have preferences among individuals."

"That's right."

The room where she sleeps is nearly empty, a concrete shell like Shael's room in the camp, apart from a lamp and a mattress with soft sheets. Kissing her isn't like kissing Coe, not even when she kisses back forcefully. It's—the thought seems bizarre, but it attaches and won't let go—it's closer to what Shael imagines kissing *them* must be like. They feel, more than they've ever felt with Coe, a confusion between self and other as their body touches hers.

She removes her own robe and undergarments, then theirs. Unlike Coe, again, in the slowness of her movements, how she engulfs Shael's smaller body as she wraps her arms around them, a nexus of softness, heat. What are they to do? They once stole away to the abandoned infirmary wing with a masculine Between whose body was in some ways like Calla's, with parts like her parts. But their energy was closer to Coe's: jagged, forceful. Happy to lead.

So is Calla, to be sure, in her fashion: guiding Shael's hands to her, placing them where she wants, whispering how she'd like to be touched. They stroke her, linger over her wetness, feel her cup their bum gingerly, as if it might break. They let her guide their mouth to her clit, obey her instructions: *Softer, a little higher.* They want to please her, are concerned they won't. Their mind is strangely almost empty, unlike when they're with Coe and in a thick atmosphere of fantasy, their suffering in the camp rewritten as pleasure. The motion of their tongue accelerates. She moans. "Keep going," she says, barely. They do. Her back arches, her legs trembling. They hope they're doing right, doing well. They await further instructions. She runs her hands through their hair, in and out of its waves. Gently tugging the scruff of their neck, she draws their face back up to hers and places a hand on their clit. Strokes them. "Tell me what you like."

What do they like? So much of their sexual excitement is tied to the performance of power: rituals of authority, of punishment, consensually enacted. But to urge sex in that direction here, in this settlement that is a living repudiation of coercive authority, feels strange. Not impossible, probably not against any named rule. But strange.

"I like what you're doing now," they murmur. "You can...keep doing that..."

"Happily. And no judgment if you want to suggest anything else." They hesitate. They're aroused.

"I like to be beaten," they whisper. "Like we are in the camp."

The motion of her hand slows but doesn't stop.

"Not for real," they add quickly. "Not by correctors. But I like to... re-enact."

She guides their hand between her legs. She's wet. They pulse their fingertips against her, trace circles. She takes small, sharp breaths.

"When I'm with him..." Shael whispers. "I...you want to hear?"

She nods, her hair trailing against Shael's small breasts.

"He strips me. He bends me over, scolds me, tells me I've broken a rule, many rules, the consequences may be dire, I'm under his control now. He punishes me the way we're punished in the camp if we transgress."

She strokes them, slowly, along the length of their clit. Observes them. "You're beautiful," she says.

They feel a flush rise to their cheeks. No one has spoken to them like this before, not really: in the camp they were made to feel their appearance was odd, they were too small, too much like a girl, but of course not a girl, never a girl, just an awkward young man. Coe made them feel desired, certainly, but in ways that were mostly non-verbal.

Their Betweenness was more or less unnameable in that place, could never surface enough to suggest its own expressible standards for beauty.

"I don't know that I could do that to someone from the camp," she says, releasing their clit, running her hands through their hair. "Beat them, I mean. Given where I come from. I think it might feel too... wrong. Though I know it'd be only play."

Both of them lie on their backs, their chests rising and falling.

"Even doing this much together..." She studies their face. "You wanted to?"

"Yes."

"Where I grew up, we were told we could have everything, everyone, we were all equals, we just had to ask. But of course we weren't all equals, even there. I don't want to take advantage. You're very new here, and you've been through a lot."

They breathe deeply. Exhale. "To be seen...the way I am, and to be wanted...and to be able to touch like this, without needing to hide..." They bring their face to hers, kiss her. "I can't believe it's real."

Gently she kisses them back. "It's real. And it's fragile."

THE COUNCIL CHAMBER IS FULL. THE COMMUNITY IS arranged, as at the previous meeting Shael attended, in a large circle with concentric layers, chairs staggered to improve sightlines.

"Violence against each other is a collective wound," Dorota says from her seat in the front row, her long white hair shimmering in the sunlight that streams through the chamber's tall, narrow windows— those few that remain, whose frames haven't been boarded up. "We feel it through the whole of our social body. It's rare now. We've worked hard to make it so. But when it erupts, we must attend to it swiftly."

Shael wonders for whose benefit this preamble is offered. It seems catered to newcomers, those unfamiliar with the settlement's forms of justice. As if sensing their thought, Calla lowers her lips to their ear, whispers: "We use these moments as a reminder of our values. Useful even for comrades who have been here a long time."

Dorota casts a glance around the circle. "It's good to see your faces."

There are murmurs of reply, nods of greeting.

"How's your injury, Natum?"

Natum, also seated in the circle's front row, has a sling around one of his arms and a brace against that same side of his torso. Even now, his face suggests openness, warmth. It melts into an easy smile as he meets

Dorota's gaze. "I've been better," he says. "But to be with you here is a pleasure."

"We meet under difficult circumstances. But to be with you here is a pleasure," she repeats. Clearly the phrase is formalized, a customary expression in Riverwish. Maybe an institution of the settlement's founders in particular; it seems to spring most naturally and most often from elders' mouths.

"Even to be with my friend Caiben today is a pleasure," says Natum, his deep voice resonant in the high-ceilinged chamber.

"Because you know you're granted power over me in this place." The voice comes from the other side of the circle.

"He has no special power over you, Caiben," says Dorota.

"He has the force of his grievance. We all know that the one who's been victimized holds the real power here."

Dorota's expression remains impassive. "Not the power to do injustice."

"Okay," says Caiben. "We've heard this. So you say."

There's a stirring around the circle, a general murmur.

"I have no hunger for injustice, my friend," Natum says.

"So you say."

"You might reckon with your own injustice before accusing others," Natum continues. "You might consider your own inability to hear another person's *no*."

"It wasn't her *no*, it was yours. You have no right to set limits on her freedom."

"You have no right to strike a comrade. For any reason."

"We'll take a moment, friends," says Dorota. "We have a process. Let's not rush."

The others fall silent. But a new tension fills the room. Shael's heart thuds; they shift in their seat. Calla squeezes their hand.

"Please make a brief statement of the circumstances first, Natum. Caiben will have a chance to do the same."

Natum hesitates for a moment, his mouth pursing, relaxing. "When they believe death might be near, men can act wrongly in their desperation. Not just men, but men worst of all, I think. I understand why my comrade attacked me—"

"For *you* to call that—"

"Wait your turn," Dorota warns Caiben, with a sharpness that feels like escalation.

"I understand why he set upon me," Natum continues. "He thought he might die in the raid. He loves Marya, I can appreciate that, I love Marya too. But our friend Caiben has always struggled with other people's boundaries. Marya had told him she and I are a closed pair, that's how we've chosen to live, and he couldn't accept it. He got this idea, built this fantasy that I was pressuring Marya into our arrangement, restricting her freedom, that she's been dying to get out. But that isn't what she says. That isn't what she tells me and I don't believe it's what she told Caiben. He hears what he wants. So when, in his desperation, in the terror of a raid, when he confronts me like I'm imprisoning his love? Like I'm trapping this woman? That's wrong. And when he swings at me with this, this club, this tube of a bicycle he's found, like he's some corrector? That's worse. He breaks my rib? Come on. Caiben, if you don't see how you bring the camp out of the camp like this, I don't know what to tell you. We all decided we weren't going to act this way out here."

The silence that falls is so total that the wind rattling the trees outside not only becomes audible, but even seems loud. Natum sits back in his chair. Shael glances at Calla, tries to read from her face whether the trial is proceeding like normal, but she gives nothing away. When, in her bed, she described how these processes unfold, they sounded peaceful, rooted in an optimism that the parties in conflict would share some basic agreement about their situation, a degree of consensus about what the harm was and who was most responsible for it. Shael hadn't imagined so much hostility straining the proceedings. In retrospect that feels naive.

"Caiben may respond, followed by other parties, including Marya if she wishes."

A gallery of eyes on Caiben. He says nothing at first, sits still, studying the floor. A few whispers, unintelligible, snake across the silence.

For a moment Shael wonders whether Caiben might just rise from his seat in the front row and leave, refuse the terms of engagement. What would happen then? What does justice look like in Riverwish when peace, or a prescribed road to it, is spurned outright? When a dangerous person refuses to comply with efforts to pacify him?

But Caiben stays where he is.

"I resent the spin," he says.

"No spin," Natum says.

"Please let Caiben respond," Dorota says.

"I resent the spin," Caiben goes on, "and I dislike knowing how you all believe it when it comes from someone you find charming. Personality rules here, doesn't it. We say there's no hierarchy, but that's not true. Charisma, that's what matters here. How well-liked you are. In the camp it mattered too, but it had limits, the power structure there was mostly independent of personality once you got beyond the low-level favour economy. But here? My word against his? I lose. And you all know it."

He pauses. The room breathes and waits on him.

"It wasn't because of Marya that I struck him. He knows that. Spin. I struck him because my dignity could no longer abide what he was doing to me, how in his violent jealousy he was using his popularity to undermine me, isolate me, make other potential lovers refuse me, I would *no longer* just absorb those blows, you think it's not violence because you can't see it? Because no scanner can find the wound? He was turning this place into a nightmare for me."

Shael glances at Calla. She's watching Natum, whose apparent calm doesn't lapse but also doesn't seem to reach his eyes.

"And where am I to go? You tell me. If I'm pushed out, if every woman and man in the settlement spurns me as a villain, if only the Betweens will tolerate my company, but in the end I can't make my life with them, because I'm unlike them, what am I to do? Wait to serve our rebellion with my death? If I'd wanted to live a shadow of a life, I could have stayed in the camp."

Murmurs around the circle.

"Where am I to go? You tell me. What am I to do?"

Caiben sits back in his chair, folds his hands in his lap. He meets no one's eye.

"You're to do as you do now," Dorota says eventually. "Enter into a process. Seek reconciliation."

"But we're assembled here only because I struck him. If I hadn't done violence, the horrible situation would just have gone on."

"You could have called a process yourself. If he was harming you."

"The harms were too subtle. No one would have believed me, or acknowledged their complicity. He's far too popular. And you know it. Even the calling of a process—how it's called, whether it's called— even this is determined by personality."

"If you had put your cynicism to the test and called a process before escalating to physical violence, you might've been surprised by how accommodating your comrades would have been."

"Maybe. Doubtful."

"When one of us does private violence because he mistrusts our methods of justice, it weakens us all."

"But if the mistrust is warranted?"

"Then that's a matter for discussion, something we all must struggle through together."

"Will you admit that Natum is far more powerful than I am?"

"He has no special authority."

"Untrue. He has no *official* authority. But he's listened to. Deferred to."

"That's a kind of power, yes. What would you have us do about it?"

"Acknowledge it."

"It's acknowledged."

"By the collective?" Caiben glances around the room. "You admit I speak the truth?"

"True or not," Dorota replies, "what you say is no justification for striking someone who struggles alongside you."

Caiben shakes his head, averts his eyes.

Shael feels warm breath at their ear. "Sometimes I worry," says Calla very softly, "that almost all we'd do in utopia is wade through endless status conflicts like this one. What else would we do there? We couldn't just have sex all the time."

They're startled by her cool, sardonic tone, but they have little time to reflect on it before a different voice echoes through the chamber.

"So tiresome."

"Marya, a moment," says Dorota. "Caiben, have you finished?"

Caiben nods.

"Marya, you are welcome."

"Don't you find this all *exhausting*?"

Natum and Caiben glance at her, then at each other. A brief circuit of whispers coils through the room. Shael looks from face to face, lingering on Marya, in the front row like the rest of those most implicated in the proceedings. Pretty, not young, with intelligent eyes. At once Shael feels the men's claims name her without seeing her. They *miss* her; she's absent from them. They make her a mere instrument by which the men jockey for prestige. A dynamic her voice rejects.

"I never desired you, Caiben. I told you this, first gently, then without ambiguity. You chose not to listen."

Natum responds with a grin, which he suppresses, barely, after a moment. If Caiben is crestfallen, his expression gives nothing away.

"But the rest of what Caiben says is true," Marya continues. "Natum's efforts to marginalize every person with a cock who desires me? Transparent. Obvious. Despicable. I've asked him to stop. I've asked you to stop," she says to Natum, from whose face mirth is draining. "And have you listened? Why should you? You do what you like, nobody challenges you. Because we all still have more of the camp in us than we admit. Too many of us still worship authority, or the appearance of authority, and it's linked in our minds to its old forms. A man. A charismatic man. A man of strength, with great appetites. 'We all decided we weren't going to act this way out here.' You say that, Natum. But look at you. Or maybe it's wrong to blame you, or only you—we give you this power. Look at *us*. Look how we're living."

For a moment nobody speaks.

"A difficult freedom is preferable to life as a prisoner," says an elder with a high, clear voice. They bear a strong resemblance to Dorota—sisters, perhaps.

"What if they're just two kinds of prison?" Marya replies.

"They're not," the elder says. "And it insults our struggle to compare them."

"I wish to end my relations with Natum," Marya says, her eyes still on the elder who answered her, but her voice addressing the crowd. "I name this in public." She turns her gaze on Natum. "For safety."

His eyes flash. He lunges out of his chair. In a blink, many sets of hands—male and female and Between, young and old—seize him. They press him back into his seat, restrain him there. He struggles briefly, grows still. He pants. All pretense of nonchalance gone.

"I wasn't inviting you to illustrate my point," Marya says, her voice shaking.

Shael's heart races. Natum's volcanic aggression rocks them. They had sensed no violence in him. Or if they'd sensed it, they'd read it as controlled, virtuous—like Coe's. Not a wild anger that could suddenly endanger a lover.

They notice now that in the moment of swift collective action to restrain Natum, there's been an equivalent closing of ranks around Marya: at least a dozen others have formed a protective ring around where she sits. It must have happened almost instantly. As if well-practised. As if this is far from the first time such manoeuvres have proven needful.

Calla rests her hand on Shael's knee. "Nothing to worry about."

And in fact the room has calmed again already. The ring around Marya remains in place but relaxes. Those who held Natum linger near him, but more casually.

"We've all heard Marya's wish, and it will be respected," says Dorota. "Secure accommodation is available if you need it."

"I wouldn't mind," says Marya, her voice still unsteady.

"Neither Natum nor Caiben will trouble you," says Dorota. "On pain of a Second Process."

The formality of the term—a *Second Process*, not just a second process—is audible to Shael. It unnerves them.

"One part of the conflict is then settled," Dorota goes on. "But not the whole of it. Natum, do you recognize the behaviour that Caiben and Marya have named? How you use your popularity to hurt others?"

"No doubt my popularity will crater after this," Natum says, almost a snarl. "You think being liked and trusted is great power? Then why's it so fragile?"

"We don't know how this process will affect your status."

"We've all seen it. In other processes, with other comrades. Just to be accused is enough." His grin is bitter. "Destroys your participant approval score."

"We have no such measure here," says Dorota.

"Might as well."

"You were the victim in this process," Caiben says.

"Not anymore, my friend. Now we're both villains."

"Neither of you is a villain," Dorota says. "Nobody here will say so."

"Their glances will," Natum says.

"It's true," says Caiben.

Calla bends her lips to Shael's ear again. "Pity us on the day when the men realize they can overthrow the council chamber's justice if they band together once more. In their arrogance and contempt."

"You didn't answer the question," Dorota says to Natum. "Do you make a weapon of your influence? Do you recognize this pattern that others have described?"

"It's not my fault if people listen to me."

"He's not going to admit it," Caiben says. "His power depends on him disavowing it."

"What do you each need to move forward in peace?"

"This process has revealed his nature to the group in ways that could be useful," Caiben says. "That may be the best result I could've hoped for."

"Then you admit our trials can be effective," Dorota says to Caiben.

"I might be overestimating how today will weaken his prestige," says Caiben. "It's not like his brutality is a surprise to most of you. It may just get explained away—because he's popular."

"You return to this one point because you have nothing else to say in your defence," says Natum.

"I'm sorry for striking you. I regret it. I still despair of other justice, but I regret it. If only because it makes me more like you."

"I'm nothing like you."

Marya laughs. Natum stirs. The protective circle around Marya closes its gaps.

"I accept his apology," Natum says, after a strained pause. "If that will help us conclude. Then I accept."

"Thank you," says Dorota. "And will you commit to not speaking ill of Caiben, or even not speaking of him at all? To end your own pattern of violence against him?"

"I will not speak of him," Natum says.

"On pain of a Second Process?" Caiben asks Dorota.

"Certainly on pain of a new trial," says Dorota.

"But not a Second Process?" Caiben repeats.

"Weak man with a taste for blood," Natum mutters.

"He violates his vow already!" says Caiben.

"You provoke me! You go out of your way to provoke me!"

"By asking for justice? For consequences if vows are broken?"

"You don't want justice, you want blood!"

"Quiet!" says Dorota.

The men fall silent.

"Does anyone else wish to speak?"

For a long time no one makes a sound. Eventually, a faint voice from the back row: "I would like to…offer…only that what they've said about Natum…I believe to be true. I've seen it. He has spoken viciously of Caiben. And of many other men."

"Not only men," says a young Between across the circle.

"And he's done worse."

"A lot worse."

"He asked me a dozen times to come to his bed."

"And me!"

"He believes a woman's refusal is a challenge. He'll never admit it, but he does."

"You don't recognize your size, Natum! Your physical size! Some of us submit to you simply because we're scared!"

"He thinks because he was a founder he's entitled to anyone he likes."

"It's exhausting!"

"Do you think we don't talk?!"

"No, he thinks he's the only one who talks."

"The fiction that you and Marya were a closed couple! The grotesque *fiction*!"

"Closed for her, maybe."

"When did he ask you to come to his bed?"

"A moment, please," says Dorota.

Everyone stops speaking.

Natum looks as if he'll vomit. His mouth hangs open, his eyes are wide. When he lifts his hands, gesturing vaguely at the circle, they tremble. "I was...supposed to be the victim here." His astonishment strikes Shael as genuine. "A man...hit me. Unprovoked."

Someone snorts.

"This wasn't supposed to be..."

"Can we consider a Second Process now?" says Caiben. "As a consequence of any further transgression?"

"Second Processes are reserved for cases where there's an intractable risk of harm to others," says Dorota. "I'm not convinced this is such a case."

"So put it to the collective," says Caiben.

"It requires the consensus of everyone besides the accused's closest intimates, and you won't get that, because I say no," says Dorota, more firmly.

"Have you never been intimate with Natum?" asks Caiben.

A deep flush swells across Dorota's cheeks and neck. "I am not among his closest intimates."

"Put it to the collective," Caiben repeats.

"You're a mob," Natum says.

Dozens of faces turn to him.

"You're a mob, that's all you are." His voice shakes. "You think you're…compassionate, you think you're some noble…deliberative body, trying to make peace…but you're a mob."

"You didn't feel that way when you believed them to be on your side," Caiben says.

"I was wrong."

"You're just unable to accept what you're hearing. The people are the people. They don't suddenly become demonic when they find fault with you."

"We should've made a procedure for sending comrades back to the camp," Natum says. The comment stirs murmurs throughout the room, which he ignores. "We should've planned for how someone could break from the group without suffering internal exile. Or worse."

"Do you have no will to make peace?" asks Dorota.

"If I'm so hated by so many…"

"Clearly there are grievances about you, serious ones, but nobody has said they hate you."

Natum flicks a hand towards Caiben. "He does. He wants a Second Process."

"He won't get it," says Dorota with finality. "Vengeance has no voice here."

"I don't want to be…I don't want to live like…"

"Like me?" says Caiben. "Like someone mistrusted and cast out? The condition you put me in, deliberately?"

"You're lucky I just absorbed the blow when you struck me," says Natum, his voice level. "I could've killed you."

Shouts burst across the room again. "Animal!" someone hollers. Several people leap to their feet.

"Be calm," Dorota says. Her voice subdues but doesn't silence the crowd. "A committee of elders without intimate attachment to the parties will convene to recommend next steps. This process isn't finished. But we adjourn for now. What's needed to restore peace?"

"His removal!" Caiben yells.

"It wouldn't hurt," says Marya.

Natum just sits where he is, his expression flat.

"He can come with us," says a voice Shael recognizes.

Daekin stands on their own, in the back row. The elder seems paler than when Shael last saw them, their face now furrowed with concern. It takes a moment for Shael to make sense of their own surprise: they'd thought Daekin, estranged from the community, wouldn't attend its public meetings—and indeed they hadn't been at the previous one. Calla also looks startled.

"We can care for him in our house until he's ready to return. As we cared for Caiben before this trial."

Dorota hesitates, observes Daekin. "You're able?"

"Yes."

She looks at Natum. "This is acceptable to you?"

Natum shrugs.

"Please reply."

"Acceptable. Fine."

"And no contact with the other parties until we reconvene."

"I have no wish to speak with them."

"Good. So we'll end. Thank you all for attending. Escorts, please."

Before anyone else stirs, Daekin approaches Natum with a group of about ten other Betweens, who have assembled with uncanny swiftness. Natum allows them to guide him from the chamber. The circle of protectors that formed around Marya escorts her out soon afterwards.

Shael turns to Calla. "Is that normal? The way that went?"

"There is no normal when it comes to trials. They're…messy."

Messy feels like an understatement.

"At least it's all in the open," Calla continues, a touch defensive. "At least these decisions are made by everyone concerned. The community as a whole. Not a handful of sadists working to serve the corporation's interests."

"What's a Second Process?"

She recoils, subtly, just for a moment, before recovering a careful neutrality. "It's a last resort. For when someone poses a danger to the community that can't be resolved through the ordinary means."

"How does it differ from the kind of process we just saw?"

"The proceedings are similar…but invested with the power of life and death."

Shael blinks.

"Do you see any prisons here?" Calla says flatly, staring at them. "Do you see anyone tasked with guarding prisoners? Any disciplinarians, *correctors*? Any barbed wire or locks on property? It would be nice to believe this is all possible because of some taming of human rapaciousness that's succeeded here in a generation. But that's a bit too optimistic, don't you think? The gentleness of most of our ways is made possible by the existence of the Second Process."

Shael's gut is constricted, aching. "By the threat of murder, you mean."

"The community isn't able to enforce exile. It would be ultimately defenceless against internal threats if it also lacked the power to impose death. In the extreme case only, of course."

"The extreme case only," Shael repeats, dazed.

"You find it to be wrong."

"I find it…unthinkable. After the experience of the camp. To inflict that on other survivors."

"Maybe reserve judgment until you've fallen into a feud with a violent person," she says. "See whether you feel horror at the thought of a Second Process then. Maybe you'll be relieved that your tormentor has reason to fear real punishment should they decide to smash your head in."

"I thought we all came to this place to escape a universe of punishment." They realize as soon as the words are out of their mouth that she personally *didn't* settle here for such reasons, or not exactly: she's never lived in those bleak corridors, every nuance of their design meant to threaten punishment or support its administration.

"You can't compare." She sounds irritated, her words clipped; Shael is reminded of the elder at the trial who made the same objection. "Such violence is a part of daily life there, no? Here it's the exceptional case. Extremely rare."

The word *rare* sends a chill through their whole body. "So it's been carried out…that penalty. Murder."

She looks at them with something like pity. "A few times. Of course."

Shael feels leaden. Glancing around the chamber, they see that at least half of those who attended the trial have now left, while those who remain are immersed in their own private conversations.

"How is it done?" they ask, without meeting her eye.

As they wait for an answer, their gaze lingers on a person across the room. They're so rattled that they don't immediately register that it's Maliez.

She sees them, too. Her eyes widen. Maliez, senior member of the Blood Moon. The only other escapee on Shael's transport who made it to Riverwish, but who's since been convalescing in Abia's care.

"Hello, stranger," she says with a warm smile, approaching.

Shael throws their arms around her. A wave of relief sweeps through them: the comfort of the familiar in a strange new place. They notice Calla studying her own hands, remote. Maybe just trying to be polite, to give the reunited comrades space. But her withdrawal is conspicuous.

Maliez looks the same as she did when they left the camp. Her tall, lean frame is as imposing as ever, unbent; her eyes are lively and defiant. She's not obviously injured or unwell. So why were they kept apart?

"I'd like some time alone with my friend, please," Maliez tells Calla.

"Of course. Where will you go?"

"To the house where I'm staying."

Calla's mouth opens, but at first she says nothing. Then: "In the west?"

"So they tell me."

"Pay attention to the path." She speaks only to Shael. "So you can find your way back."

council chamber with Maliez, both of them donning their sunglasses, the forest whispering as ever. It's so good to see her. Maliez, who's been present in Shael's life for years. Who knows Coe. With her typical assurance in her step, she leads them down roads lined with grey buildings, not the same few paths Shael has walked with Calla since they arrived in Riverwish. They pass courtyards surrounded by stone walls. The walls are broken in places, and Shael catches glimpses of houses within the yards: some apparently whole, others in ruins, heaps of rubble still surrounded by tall, useless gates.

"Who lives here?" Shael asks.

"Who lives here now, or who lived here before?"

"Both, I guess?"

"Now it's comrades, of course. Before? People rich enough to be able to afford privacy."

Abruptly the houses abate, giving way to a long field of nothing: at least a thousand paces long, just hard earth and unforgiving sky. At the end of it is a single walled house and courtyard, and beyond that another field, another isolated dwelling, another field. On the third such expanse of wind and desolation, a small figure on a bicycle races over the uneven ground. A child, Shael sees.

"They call this area the west," Maliez says. "Almost everyone who lives here is from the camp. Or their offspring." Her gaze lingers on the bicycling child. "They mistrust the Mountainers who defected. They try to stay uninvolved with them, as much as possible."

"Is there a feud? Between the west and…the others?"

"Less than a feud," she says. "But certainly a tension."

"So we were kept apart because each of the sides claimed one of us."

"They wouldn't acknowledge it if you asked. But I think so, yes."

Field after field of emptiness. Without the hiss of the forest, quiet presides. The crunch of bicycle wheels over dirt and gravel—they see several bikes now, with both child- and adult-sized riders—can be heard from a long distance.

"After the close confinement of the camp, many who settled here wanted something different. Space. Even at the cost of loneliness."

They reach the edge of a field bordered not by a house but by a sharp descent into a wooded ravine. They walk alongside it, tracing the slope's edge. At the bottom of the ravine, half-obscured by trees: steel tracks.

"One of a pair of rail lines in or near the settlement," Maliez says. "Both officially out of service. The line in the east, some distance from our inhabited area, connects the mountains with the camp."

"And this one here?"

"Runs south." She hesitates. "Far to the south."

It takes Shael a moment to suspect her meaning.

"The power games that allow this place to survive are almost unmappable. Supposedly the dissident Mountainers downplay them, since they like to take credit for the settlement's survival. But the truth is that none of this would be possible without the support of Magent."

The tracks glint in the sunlight.

"It's not inaccurate to say this place, this whole experiment in living, is a pawn in the long cold war between the two corporations," Maliez continues. "A splinter in Flint's side, a drain on its resources, and a challenge to its authority, which Magent finds expedient to support. Riverwish is also more than that, of course. But if both Flint and Magent were to decide it'd be in their shared interest to crush us, every person here would be dead within a week."

"Is there any way that someday we could be…independent?" Shael asks. "Free of both corporations? With enough power to shape our own future?"

"Some believe it's possible. Others don't, but are trying to live decent lives anyway."

"And you?"

Maliez hesitates. And with an ambiguous shake of her head, she leads them down into the ravine.

They didn't see the house at the bottom of the ravine, nestled amid the trees, until they were almost right in front of it. Inside it's barely furnished, like most of the other dwelling places in Riverwish that Shael has visited. But it's spacious. In the common room at the back of the house, one wall is all windows, through which Shael can see the sway of green foliage, train tracks just visible through gaps in the trees. The house reminds them of the Betweens' gathering place that Calla showed them, also hidden amid wilderness. That refuge. But the atmosphere here is altogether different.

The others who pass by or linger in the common area look rugged. Mostly they're lean, hair untamed, robes the worse for wear. They share some of Maliez's demeanour: no-nonsense, experienced, alert. The one called Lea, who sits with Shael and Maliez, embodies subtle shades of those qualities and is also clearly distinct from the others in the room. Though her skin is a deep olive or light brown, a tone common enough among the camp's inhabitants—it reminds Shael of their own mother's complexion—her eyes are a rare, intense blue. Her robe is just like the others', even less conspicuous than some, a plain tan colour—but her poise transforms it, makes it seem somehow ornamental, a ritual garment. She's around Maliez's age, maybe a little younger.

"And you live here now?" Shael asks.

"I go back and forth," Lea says. "But mostly I'm here."

Her voice is soft, with an accent distinct from those of the mountains and the camp: lightly lilting, the edges of consonants dulled. Shael was struck by the unusual cadences of that accent from the moment Lea called to them and Maliez in the ravine outside. A warm hello, words of welcome for Shael, and an invitation to step inside this house and get to know one another. Maliez's glance said they mustn't refuse. Couldn't risk offending this executive of the corporation reputed to be the most brutal on the planet. Not a dissident, not someone who escaped Magent to forge a freer life, but a paid and provisioned officer of that organization, as Lea has spelled out for them. Why trust someone such as this person over the defectors from the mountains, as the comrades in the west apparently do? Shael can't understand it.

"How long have you been…"

"Supporting this place?" Her tone is matter-of-fact, not boastful or combative. "Since its inception. We sent a force to protect the founders."

"So Flint knows. It knows you're here."

"Of course. That's partly why Flint is cautious about attacking this place, why it does so symbolically and not…more effectively. It's aware we have the power to retaliate, and it doesn't want to breach our treaty while it's not in a position of strength. Which it is not." Her smile is kind, and chilling. "Flint also knows several of its own mountain brats are here, and vulnerable to indiscriminate attack. Jan Oost doesn't wish to bomb his own daughter, much as he might like to whip her."

"They don't whip anyone in the mountains," Maliez says, her tone withering. "Such treatment isn't fit for human beings. Only for the animals in the camp."

"We don't whip animals either, in the south," Lea says. "Human or non-human."

"Don't you," Shael says.

"Keep in mind that everything you've heard about Magent has been run through the filter of Flint's propaganda. I won't claim our public has the degree of self-determination that your friends do here. But we're much more honest than Flint about what we are and what we offer."

"What are you? What do you offer?"

"We ask for labour. In return we provide safety, shelter. We don't lecture anyone about how they're free or happy. We don't build a culture out of torture and call it discipline. Nor do we hide the hierarchies that exist. We formalize them, we create predictable rules for them. We make the best of our difficult circumstances."

"Sounds a lot like Flint," says Shael.

"In some respects. But you might've noticed that life here, outside of corporate confines, isn't exactly easy. Even with the support of Magent and your friends from the mountains. Not everyone wants to lead a life of rebellion, where every minor detail of survival is a struggle. That sounds exhausting to me, frankly. I'd rather others build up a framework that I can accommodate myself to, as long as it's not terrible. But maybe I'm just lazy."

Again that smile: so warm, so apt to send ice down Shael's spine. They think of the constant, universal fear in the camp, the beatings, the disappearances. The lines of worry on their mother's face, etched in part by years of concern that the authorities would discover her child's Betweenness. "It *is* terrible," they say.

"I suppose terrible is relative," Lea says.

How do they all trust this person?

"Flint is more sadistic than most, it's true," she goes on. "Strada refused to trade with them for a long time, supposedly on principle."

"Strada?"

"A corporation far away. In a very narrow, very isolated safe zone. They didn't trade with us either during that period. At first everyone wondered at it, we couldn't understand how they survived. It was destabilizing, their apparent autonomy. Shook the new world system.

Then we learned they had found a strategic mineral deposit—found and soon exhausted it. And so they resumed relations with us, very deferential, very polite. You probably learn little about the world system in Flint's camp?"

Shael glances sidelong at Maliez, who looks unruffled. Maybe she's heard all this before. But Maliez's face seldom gives her thoughts away.

"Flint and Magent aren't alone on the planet, you know," Lea continues. "This is among the largest of the habitable zones, usually spared extremes of flood and drought, but of course it's not the only such territory. There are seven corporations, along with a number of quasi-independent satellites. None of our economies are fully self-sufficient. We trade. Not for profit, in the old sense. But not purely for utility, either. Also for position. Flint and Magent have long dominated the world system because of our mines in particular, among other advantages. Every corporation needs batteries to store power, you see, whatever our other differences. You need some reliable power source for the cameras and food-synthesizing systems in your prison camps, your enormous weapons of war that swarm across the plains like the locusts of the old story. Flint and Magent have been locked in a stalemate for an age because we have access to fundamentally the same resources. We have no material need to trade with each other. And in our development overall, we're too evenly matched for either party to feel assured of victory in open warfare. So instead we have caution, and scheming. A kind of peace."

It's as if she's painted a far shore to the ocean, a world beyond. As if by painting it she's brought it to life. Shael is exhilarated. And unaccountably livid.

"Why are you telling me this?"

"Because nobody's ever told you, and you deserve to know. You're not a child. You should understand the world you're part of. And its limitations." She presses her lips together, into a razor-thin line. "Notwithstanding its fanciful name, Riverwish isn't a paradise woven out of principle and desire. It's part of a system. A rational part, with rational limits."

"You mean we can never have real power," Shael says, heeding the kind of defiant impulse they spent years training themselves to quiet.

"You can have as much power as you're able to build within the world system, and that system is incapable of rewarding the virtue of your settlement's social ideas alone. Power belongs to those who control the planet's remaining wealth."

"You're saying we're condemned to exist forever as debris tossed about by the struggle between corporations."

She smiles. "You haven't had much freedom to study the history of our last centuries. It illustrates rather starkly how the need to survive can place a ceiling on more ambitious projects."

"And how powerful forces will use fears about bare survival to run more ambitious projects into the ground," Shael replies, surprising even themselves. They recognize in their words the language of the Blood Moon, arguments and rhetoric that for years they've heard Coe and the others advance so eloquently, but which, back in the camp, seldom sprang from their own mouth.

Maliez, too, seems startled by Shael. The two share a tense glance. Shael feels Maliez's eyes lingering on them as they turn back to Lea.

"So Magent supports us but is pessimistic about us," Shael says. "You believe the settlement can't succeed on its own terms."

"What would that success look like?" Lea asks, almost as if she wants to know.

"Freedom and power to shape our own destiny. No more camps or corporations. Their resources placed under our control."

"I consider it unlikely, given the underlying environmental conditions," says Lea, her face all but motionless.

"You mean the underlying arrangements of power."

"We can continue this conversation later," Maliez says abruptly, as if she's become concerned that Shael's provocations might cross a line, seed a tension that would be complicated to resolve.

But Lea seems unbothered. "You attended the trial today, yes? Did it strike you as a realistic model of justice? One that could resolve conflict on a mass scale? Conflict in a very large community, I mean. The autonomy you want, how does it look when it needs to organize a million lives? Isn't it worth trading a little freedom for a lot of ease?"

"It's never just a little freedom that's lost, not for most of us. And how much ease do we have when we live under constant threat of violence?"

"If you think you can make something better, you're welcome to try."

"This is an attempt to make something better, this, here, and you know that you'd join Flint in bombing it out of existence if it were no longer useful to you."

Her smile is as immobile as a statue's. "But it is useful to us."

"For now."

Maliez clears her throat. "I think we should continue on our way."

"A pleasure to meet you," Lea says. "I appreciate your challenges, I really do. It supports my theory that Flint's forms of discipline just don't work. You can't make a spectacle of punishment and expect people to be docile out of fear, people don't work like that, they just become subtler in their rebellions, and more enraged. No, better simply to leave people to do as they want, within certain tolerable parameters, and if they break the rules too often, you don't fuss about it, you don't make a show and let your friends work out their sex kinks on them. You just kill them."

Shael can't find their breath.

"That's the principle underlying the *compassionate* model of justice here as well," Lea adds. "And honestly, that part of it is good. That part works."

Seeing that Shael is going to cause trouble if they stay any longer, Maliez places her hand on their shoulder. "Thanks for your time," she says to Lea.

Agitated, Shael lets themselves be drawn out of their seat and led from the room.

"How do they trust her!" Shael blurts once they're far enough away, or almost. "How can any of us possibly trust her!"

Maliez motions for them to lower their voice. "What choice do we have?" And she dons her sunglasses and leads them down the hall, out of the house.

The ravine is enveloping, its slopes steep on each side, bushes and trees in thick proliferation across it, save for the lane the train tracks run through. Maliez guides them down a trail hewn out of the wilderness, which winds to the tracks' clearing. The sky above them, viewed from the tracks, is a long alley, bordered by the trees' canopy on each side. As Shael's gaze follows that strip of sky to where it vanishes, narrowing to the horizon, a dark object appears against the hazy blue. Gradually it draws closer. Soon it's near enough to be seen more clearly: a silver cylinder, with short, sharp wings.

"Wave hello," says Maliez.

The drone passes over them without slowing. It's unsettling; Shael half expects it to fire a weapon, release some toxic substance. They feel a flash of relief that their face is partly concealed by their hood and sunglasses. But the drone just speeds on, along the line of sky above the tracks, curving as the line does, soon out of sight.

"Who sent it? Flint or Magent?"

"Magent doesn't need to send drones," Maliez says. "It has its people here."

Abruptly they remember the wounded comrade they saw in the infirmary hall, the argument at the settlement's meeting before the raid. A voice from the crowd: *There's a spy!*

"And Flint?" they ask. "Has it ever infiltrated this place?"

"In the first wave of arrivals, yes. There was a spy among the defectors from the mountains. She did a lot of damage. Enabled murderous raids."

"But she was found out."

"Yes."

"And fled back to the mountains?"

Maliez doesn't respond.

"It's happening again, isn't it," Shael says. "Another spy."

"That's the fear. Dorota and a few others have been tasked with investigating. But nobody knows who would be sabotaging their comrades this way, or why. Relationships run deep here…even if a spy weren't directly endangering themselves, they'd almost certainly be risking the lives of others they care about. Kin, close friends. And if Riverwish starves because we can't restock, the spy starves too."

"Unless they're from the mountains…and could return there." Shael hesitates. Trees whisper in the light breeze. "Or from Magent."

"The spy knows things that Lea doesn't, can't. Details of forays that aren't shared with everyone in the settlement, let alone with Magent people. And most of the Mountainers have been here almost from the start. They've got the same close relationships as anyone else in Riverwish. The only relative newcomer among them is your friend Calla, and her arrival long predates the ambushed forays."

Even as Maliez minimizes the possibility, it chills them.

"You can see why investigating a possible infiltration is tricky," she goes on. "In a community built on mutual aid, trust. We just keep our eyes open, I guess."

Shael kicks at a cluster of small stones between ties of the tracks. Drained at the thought of fear and mistrust coursing through this place, too.

"Anyway," Maliez says, watching them with what might be concern—it's hard to read her expression through her dark glasses, the light flaring off them. "I know you must be impatient for news about Coe. We're going to try again to bring him out as soon as possible. His position in the camp is just too unsafe."

Shael's heart thuds. "But he's okay?"

"We don't think they know he was on that transport with us—our guards did their work. But Flint seems to have some idea that he's organizing people in the camp, he's a leader, and they hope to scare him into stopping without turning him into a martyr. Once they realize that'll never succeed, it's over. So we need to get him out before that happens."

"I want to be there when he arrives. I'll go to meet his transport."

"You have no combat training."

"So I'll train."

"You can't protect him."

"I can be there with him. I can share the risks."

"We're talking about armed confrontation. If you care about his safety, you should leave that to experienced comrades."

"A confrontation like what happened with our transport? That wasn't how it was supposed to go, was it. That was one of the ambushes."

Maliez hesitates. Her robe ripples in the wind. "Yes."

"How do we know it won't happen again? When Coe comes out?"

"There are no guarantees. He's aware of this. But he can't stay there."

They feel caged by the knowledge that there's nothing they can do to keep him safe. For the first time in a while, they're hit by a wave of frustration that Coe is Coe: rebellious, charismatic, a target for retaliation by the camp's authorities. They find themselves half wishing it had been given to them and Coe to lead a quiet life in the camp, alongside others doing the same—however restricted, however compromised. They also recognize that such a life could never have satisfied either of them. Could never have been safe for the two of them as a couple, or for Shael as a Between. To know even a shadow of peace in the camp, Shael would've had to be born a different person.

"You do so much just by being here," Maliez says, as if guessing the direction of their thoughts. "By being who you are. And surviving. That's a kind of militancy in itself."

A familiar idiom for speaking about Betweens, in whispers, among those in the camp who sympathize with them. *Your very survival is an act of resistance.* Shael has always found these sentiments a little trite. They didn't choose to be what they are. So much would've been easier for them were they gender-determinate. It would've chafed them less to be integrated into the camp's disciplinary gender matrix, with its refusal to license any but "mixed sex" matches, and its assignment of men and women to different labour tasks: heavy physical labour for the men, lighter physical labour divided between men and women, more technical healing and education work for men, less specialized healing and child-rearing work for women. Nor was the problem just their own powerful feelings of alienation when they were identified as a man for administrative or other social purposes. Throughout all their years in the camp, it was well-known that even Betweens who hadn't been officially discovered as such by the authorities were punished for their differences in a thousand subtle ways. Extra scrutiny. More noxious labour assignments. An awareness that they could be victimized— by other participants as well as by guards and correctors—with even greater impunity than most. That whatever violence and humiliation befell them would feel to the gender-determinates like a foregone conclusion, regrettable but unsurprising. *He's always been an odd one, after all.* Was it *brave* to exist in that atmosphere? What other options were there, besides suicide? Is it really an act of resistance just to want to stay alive? When they contrast this will to survive with Coe's militancy, the way he risks life and freedom to fight the oppressive conditions that afflict everyone in the camp, they're embarrassed by the comparison.

The rails trace the gradual bend of the ravine. The sun is starting to sink below the trees' canopy. Eventually Maliez leads them off the tracks and onto the ravine's far side, away from the centre of the settlement. A path cuts through the tangle of green growth, curls upwards.

"Do you miss the camp at all?" Shael asks as they clamber over a log. "Your kin there, for example?"

Maliez keeps moving. "I don't have much kin left. Most were killed when our group was hit. They were involved, you know, it wasn't just retaliation for my activities," she adds, as if to reassure Shael about the safety of their own relations. "I come from a revolutionary family."

It startles them to hear Maliez speak so bluntly of tragedy, the bloodshed that followed the defeat of the organization whose survivors helped to form the Blood Moon. "I'm sorry."

"It was a long time ago." She sweeps a branch from her path, holds it to one side as Shael passes. "I have a son. They took him from me when my approval score was downgraded. To keep me from extending my influence over him, they said. But also just to punish me. He lives in the group zone for parentless children. I get information about him from a comrade who works there. He's also why I fight. I have no other way to be reunited with him."

Shaken, Shael watches her. She just keeps moving.

"How old is he?"

"Ten."

The path crests, the trees part. They stand at the edge of another wide, flat field. Another house is visible in the distance. Rolling towards it, along a road at the field's far edge, is a figure on a bicycle. The air shimmers in the heat.

Shael and Maliez cross the field. As they approach the house, Shael sees the cyclist has dismounted and is leaning against her bike, watching them. Waiting for them. They recognize her: Abia.

"Time to rejoin your own?" she says as they draw near, with a warmth that seems genuine. "Welcome to the west."

The house is smaller than the one at the bottom of the ravine, more private dwelling than communal space. It's noticeably more furnished than most of the other living places in Riverwish that Shael has seen: delicate cloth hangings on the walls, many comfortable chairs, books on shelves. Plants. One room is dedicated almost entirely to wooden sculptures, humanoid and animal and abstract. Against a wall there, beneath a shuttered window, a long desk is covered with carving instruments, wood shavings, illustrated pages torn from books.

"Surprised to see a real home?" Abia says. "Not all of us want to live like atoms careening around a science experiment."

"Flint doesn't raid the west," Maliez explains, standing behind Shael in the doorway of the sculpture workshop. "It doesn't dare. It knows Magent's people are here. So those who choose to dwell here can be more rooted."

On the house's main floor, as in many of the houses Shael has visited in the settlement, a long hallway opens onto a wide, light-filled lounge. There, a tall, dark-skinned person with short-cropped hair sits reading. The child in their lap is no more than eight or nine years old, possibly younger.

"This is Sarone," Abia says. "And the small one she holds is Potenza."

A shiver dances through Shael at the sound of their mother's name.

"Welcome," says young Potenza.

Shael has seen children in Riverwish: blurs of motion on bicycles, or small figures around a circle in the council chamber. But they haven't been introduced to a child here until now. They find the experience uncanny. How can this outpost, so provisional, so vulnerable, have been the birthplace of a new generation?

"She was born in this house," says Abia, affirming the impossible. "She has heard stories of the camp. It's like a dream to her. She can't believe it exists."

There is a strange moment during which Shael is aware of someone weeping before they realize that it's them. They feel Maliez's hand on their back, guiding them to a soft couch. The grief that rocks them is total. All those years in the camp, the secrecy with Coe, their mother's terror, the other parent they never met, siblings who couldn't be told of their Betweenness lest they give them away, subject them to beatings, isolation, death. *It's like a dream to her. She can't believe it exists.*

"Are they sad?" asks Potenza.

The heat of the centre courts on celebration days. Those courts' ghost-stench of rotting flesh, imagined residue of all those who'd been murdered by exposure on that scorching concrete. Surveillance units in nearly every corridor: all will be known, judged, punished. The corruption of the personality under such conditions. Denunciations of participants by participants, sexual bribery of guards, atrophy of the capacity to even *imagine* a less violent, less fearful way of living. How it all became so *normal*. And how anyone who questioned that normalcy became immediately suspect, not just to the overseers but even to their own family, their workmates. Generations who'd known only that mass suffocation of human potential—so many generations that such misery began to seem like simply a fact of life, the best that could be hoped for.

She has heard stories of the camp. It's like a dream to her.

Their sobs ignite more sobs.

"We'll get you something to eat and drink when you're ready," Sarone says, her voice mellow, deep.

"Do you miss your home?" the child asks. "Is that why?"

Gasping, Shael shakes their head.

"It's a lot to process all at once," Sarone says. "Everything they know has been spun in circles, in not much time at all."

"Decompression sickness," Shael says, smiling weakly, their voice a rasp. "Surfacing too fast."

"What's that?" Potenza asks.

"Something they used to say when the oceans were alive."

An image from an unlicensed text, a pamphlet Shael read years ago, returns to them: an annotated drawing of how worsening ocean acidity, caused by human industry, eroded the shells and skeletons of creatures who lived beneath the waves. *Don't surface too quickly, but surface before it's too late.*

Abia lowers herself to the couch beside Shael and Maliez, so they're all seated together. She takes Sarone's hand. "I know you're overwhelmed. But we feel we have much to be glad of, and we want to share that with you. We've been very happy here."

"I sense that," Shael says, barely.

"There have always been people among us—comrades, call them what you will—who have devoted themselves to the collective decisions of the community, the administration of justice. And there have always been those who see such business as necessary but a chore. Who choose to focus on educating themselves and the young, making beautiful artworks, caring for their closest relations."

"Also many who attempt to strike a balance," Sarone adds.

"Right, but in the west," Abia goes on, "there's a long tradition of— do you think this is true?—I was going to say, a tradition of a certain skepticism towards the official politics of Riverwish."

"That's true," Sarone says. "A certain skepticism, yes. Those from the mountains have always had too much influence there. As have militants, in general."

"And they make a fetish of it, they do, they really believe the work of making the future is about obsessing over how to produce a justice that's *the opposite of the camp's*, and I won't say it comes full circle, but—"

"No, certainly—"

"But not everyone wants to live like that. Freedom has to mean more than a civic obligation to spend all your time administering freedom."

Maliez laughs. "We used to joke in the camp, in our group, that we wouldn't know what to do with ourselves once we were free. Our whole identities had been built around the struggle. And if the struggle were to stop existing because we won? Would we go mad, or invent new kinds of struggle just to keep ourselves occupied?" She glances at Shael, who's calmed, though their cheeks are still damp. "It wasn't a very funny joke, in retrospect."

"You can stay with us for a while," Abia says to Shael. "If you'd like. You must be exhausted from your first days here, you've seen so much."

"Here you can rest," says Sarone, "as your friend has been resting. Recover your strength."

"I'd like that," says Shael.

The wind, howling across the flatness by the house, sounds like an ancient, melancholy animal.

"Food? Potenza, lead the way."

TIDES AND DUST

HOW DOES TIME MOVE IN RIVERWISH? HOW DOES
it flow over the flatness of the west, where the sunset announces its
intentions hours in advance? Or through the ruins of the ancient town
reclaimed by forest, where the community meets to deliberate over
questions of justice, and the food hall echoes with laughter, and raids
smash the peace of night? How does this compare to the time of the
camp, a regularity that grinds, an unstable blend of tedium and menace? In the ravine with Potenza and Sarone, picking wild berries that
must never be eaten but can be ground into dye for their robes, it seems
to Shael that the time of Riverwish—at least in the west—intimates
infinity. You feel you'll live it forever, and that this perpetuity could be
desirable. Whereas the repetition of the camp is ruled by death. You feel
it will go on forever and also at any moment you might die. Time slows
there to an agonizing limp, while in Riverwish, in the west, time races
around the individual body's slowness. They've been picking berries
together for an hour and now it's winter, temperate and windy. They've
been preparing food, assembling the bounty of ingredients the Magent
people deliver to their door—odd, fraught gestures of support that
remind Shael a little too much of rations deliveries in the camp—and
now Potenza is perceptibly older, barrelling through a growth spurt. A
bicyclist flies across the field; Abia has finished a sculpture; it's spring.
A patter of rain, then a torrent.

Many hours are dedicated to educating Potenza. Abia and Sarone regard this as their primary task, an attitude that Maliez and Shael absorb. From time to time, Sarone suffers from intense headaches; when these appear, the household reconstitutes itself around tending to her and caring for Potenza while Sarone can't. They wash their robes and undergarments in the creek in the ravine, which is flowing again for the season. Deep wells, purification bottles and tablets, stories of when freshwater was everywhere abundant, long before their grandparents were born: this is what they have, and they're grateful for it.

Coe is never far from Shael's mind. Thoughts of him tend to be most overwhelming late at night and first thing in the morning. Whether he's still safe, what his life has been like in the time since Shael has seen him, whether he will in fact join them in Riverwish soon—the plan to bring him out again has met with delay after delay. Whether they'll ever again touch each other. There's so much Shael loves about Coe—his generosity and bravery, his kindness, the rage that rises in him at the sight of cruelty—but their longing for him wends back always to a sense-memory of his body, their bodies together, a craving for scent and touch. Gentle touch and painful. How his touch—both kinds of it—makes them feel seen, held. They ask Maliez whether they might send a message to him in the camp, and even perhaps receive a message back; she discourages the idea, warns that it would create too many dangers. They drop it. Important to know he's safe, but words aren't really what they want.

Abia's sculptures proliferate. She welcomes Shael to watch her at her work if it should interest them, an invitation Shael accepts more and more often. They sit beside her on her workbench as she hunches over a wooden whale, refining its features with a small blade, consulting an illustration on a torn-edged page. "There's a story I love about a man who's swallowed by an animal like this one," she says, not lifting her gaze from her work. "In an old book that's still read in Magent lands. The man in the story is told he must serve as a prophet, he has an important mission, but he doesn't want it, he flees from it.

He suffers misfortunes and ends up in the belly of a whale. Eventually he escapes and delivers the prophecy, but I always found that disappointing. Why not continue to live in the whale, if you're permitted to survive that way? Such simplicity and calm! Not everyone needs to be a prophet." Shael can't tell how serious she's being. "In the original text of that book," she goes on, "the whale was both male and female. Its gender changed over the course of the story, without explanation. I like that."

Shael visits the Betweens' house often. They sit with Bradoch, the pianist, and with Alodia, another young feminine Between, with whom they felt an instant affinity when the two met in the house during the driest week of winter. Alodia has hair that's thick like Shael's, and like Shael they're slender; they resemble each other more than a little. Despite their youth, Alodia is not new to Riverwish but came of age here. Their mother, escaping the camp, brought her vulnerable child with her. It's some time before Alodia shares with Shael their mother's fate: how she died in a raid, blocks of the roof slamming into the floor just a few paces from Alodia's sleeping body. How for years Alodia felt they should've been the one who died, an irrational guilt that's never fully left them. "In a sense, most of us are orphans here," they say to Shael one afternoon. "But some of us more than others."

The tenderness that courses between them and Shael is immediate, instinctive. Alodia serves in a bicycle workshop and is frequently absent from the house, but when they're there, often they ascend with Shael to one of the bedrooms. A subtle blue-and-purple patch on Alodia's robe, cross-hatched with fine black lines: they desire feminine and androgynous people, and they prefer to be dominated. (In the west, such signalling is widely considered a frivolous, decadent game. Shael wears no patch.) To be with another feminine Between has such an ease to it, a familiarity, that Shael can almost forget they'd never experienced it before their arrival in Riverwish. When they're naked together, soft bodies wrapped around each other, clits growing firmer in each other's hands, Shael is surprised by how little needs to be said. Just the nuances of their desire. *Press harder there, please. I*

prefer not to be touched there. You can add another finger if you want?
Sometimes the piano's song drifts up to where they lie, sets a mood,
masks their cries.

No one reacts when they return to the common room together,
the shine of their skin betraying them. Bradoch is protective of them
both. All the Betweens look after each other, at least in principle.
Intergenerationally, with care expressed in both directions. Bradoch
recounts how it was in the camp in their youth: the subterfuges necessary to procure masculinizing endos or clothes, or to visit a lover.
The stories sound like they could describe Shael's own life, so little has
changed in the camp. "When I arrived here," Bradoch says, deep creases
etched along the corners of their eyes as they smile, "I wondered how
I would feel in a society where everyone wears the same style of clothing." It's true: all the Betweens in the room wear robes that, while dyed
variously to express individual taste, don't differ by gender. "But look at
us. We're all dressed the same, more or less. But you know when you're
among us, don't you."

At first Shael says nothing to Daekin, though they're always aware
when the elder is near. Then Daekin begins to wave from their garden
as Shael approaches. It makes Shael's heart hammer. They wave back,
hurry into the house. "Do they ever come inside?" Shael asks Alodia
as the two of them lie together. "They're always out there when I visit."
Alodia caresses Shael's bottom, teases their lips across Shael's neck.
"They come in when they want to. They don't usually just relax, though.
When they're among us, they're often struggling with an outcast."

Shael thinks of Natum, the man ostracized during the trial they
witnessed. They've seen him walking the halls of the Betweens' house,
restless, shrouded in gloomy introspection. He never spends time in
the common room, keeps mostly to his bedroom on the second floor.
Many of the Betweens visit him, sit with him for long hours. Shael has
asked them about this practice. Is it a duty incumbent on Betweens in
particular? Nobody forces them to help the community in this way,
the others tell Shael, but a norm has developed in Riverwish—that
Betweens are able and willing to support comrades' healing in such

a fashion—and the practice has replicated itself without anybody demanding that it must. Some trace its origins to the fact that Betweens themselves have long been disproportionately targeted with ostracism and subtler forms of exclusion. The horror of such experiences that they've developed as a result; the empathy they feel with those cast out. "We try to walk with these people to the point where they're no longer a danger to others," Bradoch has told Shael. "And not a danger to themselves, which is at least as great a risk after a person loses their world." When the process is successful enough that the outcast can be fully reintegrated into the community, as is frequently the case—the settlement's vulnerability and internal interdependence leave little room for failure in these efforts—the experience can be a profound thrill. In those moments, such work feels to Shael like the very heart of the revolutionary enterprise. Daekin is reputed to be among the most committed to this labour, though Shael has never seen them at it: to help build trust between the interlocutors, the struggle tends to be conducted in private.

Daekin waves to Shael from the garden. Shael waves back and hurries on. They wave back and slow. They wave back and can't take another step, can't breathe. "A beautiful day!" Daekin calls to them. Daekin's voice sounds like their own. Of course it doesn't. The day is like every other. It is not beautiful. It is so beautiful they can't bear it. "The flowers grow quickly in this season! A marvel!" Daekin is so cheerful. Shael feels that if they open their own mouth to reply, their voice will be morbid by comparison. "You might linger with me in the garden sometime, if you'd like," Daekin says, more subdued, still warm. "I consider it one of the more pleasant corners of our little strip of fragile life." They can't accept this invitation. They want to, desperately. They feel they're being absurd: Daekin may well be just a stranger, an unusual figure even among the Betweens but otherwise unconnected to Shael, not a fit occasion for such flights and craters of feeling. They've developed a hunch, without proof. It's not as if Daekin seems like anyone's parent. They seem to exist outside of animal processes of generation: unborn, unbirthing, just there.

When Shael's thoughts turn to their lost parent, they can summon no crisp image to which they might compare a new friend. Their mother would grow distant when Shael would ask for descriptions of their other parent. She avoided the subject—so as not to provoke Tann, her rematch, though perhaps for other reasons as well. Perhaps because it was a tender point, an abyss of memory. Shael didn't often resent their other parent's absence: it was just another loss-thick fact of life in a sea of many. But they'd also had no idea their other parent might've been a Between, someone who could've stood with them, helped guide them in that part of their experience where they felt most alien. What they do remember of their absent parent is ghostly, more a feeling than a glimpse: a presence that took up almost no space. Fragments of song, maybe a lullaby: *And the sheep wound their way to the river, left their shepherd far behind…* They seem to remember their absent parent as slight and uncommonly pale. As if there were some Mountainer in their genetic mix; as if one of their ancestors had belonged to the ruling caste and been imprisoned as a dissident. Daekin is pale, if sun-darkened. But Shael's spectral memory of their parent may not be reliable.

They visit Calla, on occasion. Itinerant as ever, each time she's in a different apartment or house, with few possessions. Sometimes another lover of hers is there. She doesn't invite Shael to bed; there's no acknowledgement that they ever shared an intimacy of that sort. She seems even a bit wary of them now that they've settled in the west, though she never outright faults them for it. She asks many questions. *Do they speak ill of us? Is there active hostility from the west towards the rest of us? Why does Abia always look at me as if she wants to yank my hair? Do they actually praise Magent, or is it just a calculated alliance?* Shael answers as simply as possible: those in the west don't go out of their way to speak ill of anyone; they feel mistrust but not active hostility towards other comrades; Abia never mentions Calla in particular (a lie they're not entirely certain why they tell); those in the west have no love for Magent but accept its support because it lets them live the way they choose. "And when the time comes to rise up against Magent as against Flint?" Calla asks. "Where will they stand? Do they really think their peace can last? The sole reason their houses aren't bombed is that Flint finds it expedient to preserve the treaty with Magent. That won't always be the case. The lines will shift again. At some point those comrades will need us, and we'll need them."

Not for the first time, Shael wishes Coe were there to interpret, clarify the situation, with his acute instincts for how power moves. "We're bringing him out again soon," Calla tells them in the food hall one evening. They're both sitting with Hans, the former executive from the mountains. "I've been hearing that for a long time now," Shael says. "The call was to bring him out as soon as possible and no sooner than is safe," Calla replies. "It hasn't been safe." She doesn't elaborate. "We can't find the spy," Hans says, more whimsically than seems appropriate. "Our supply forays keep getting brutalized. It's becoming much more than a nuisance." Shael glances at Calla. She seems remote. "Anyway," she goes on, looking past them, "if you still want to be on the team that meets his transport"—Shael has dropped hints that they do want this—"you should train. I can arrange it. Just let me know." Hans drinks deep from his mug, which holds Mezin, a sweet beverage reserved for celebration days in the camp. "Calla will be on the team," he says. "She doesn't feel she's doing enough if she's not risking her tits." She rolls her eyes. "A true spirit of adventure," he goes on, his tone caustic in a way Shael dislikes.

Why does Shael feel the need to risk their own, comfortable as their life is with Abia and Sarone, Potenza and Maliez? They find such pleasure in sitting with the others for hours in the evenings, discussing their days, joining Potenza in the simple games she invents. "I'm thinking of a word that rhymes with my name. Clue: it's a nickname we give a certain animal!" Shael's bed in the house in the west is soft and wide. Inevitable, maybe, that they start to imagine what it would be like to share that bed with Coe. They ask their hosts whether he might stay with them when he arrives. "He's welcome," Abia replies. "Of course you're also free to leave together if you'd prefer, make a home as we've done here." She shares a warm, complicit glance with Sarone.

The more Shael has learned about how the two of them came together, the more Shael has come to love their love. Sarone and Abia had been aware of each other in the camp, lived on the same hub block, but though they stole glances at each other, they never spoke there for more than a few minutes at a time. After arriving in Riverwish, separately, they both fell into intimate relationships with men. And stole glances at each other, perhaps more often than they'd done in the camp, but still hardly spoke. Later, when Potenza was an infant, Sarone's partner fell ill and died, and the community—especially those in the west—rallied to support the mother and child. Abia became a regular presence in the house, a friend and comrade who'd help with child care and cleaning, as many other neighbours did.

But whenever Abia was there, Sarone would sit with her, just talking, after Potenza had gone to sleep, and abruptly they'd discover it was almost daybreak. They'd speak of the settlement's customs and tensions, the politics of the camp they'd left behind. How they'd each always loved women, but it was a truth that had never felt possible to live, even once they were free of the camp and could follow their desires as they wished. They'd carried that feeling of impossibility out of the camp with them. So when they kissed for the first time, it felt impossible. The next morning, they literally couldn't believe it; each asked the other, sincerely, to confirm it hadn't been a dream. And by the morning after that, it felt impossible that they'd ever done otherwise. It felt as though they'd been doing this, what they were doing now, together, all their lives.

"Our life now would've once seemed unimaginable to both of us," Sarone says, sitting with Abia on cushions in the house's main room, drawing small circles with her fingertips on her partner's back. "For Abia especially, I'd say. She was always floating around. Weren't you? Before us? Always looking for a place to be." Abia's smile is faint. A little distant. "I hardly remember the time before us," she says.

But on other occasions, Abia has attested to what Sarone describes: a certain rootlessness, the opposite of her life now. In the camp she'd lost her parents early; she had no siblings there, as far as she could tell. She was something of a loner by nature as well, and perhaps it was her sense that she had nothing and no one to lose that made her a militant of unusual courage, reputed to take risks few of her peers would consider. Though Flint never seemed to cast its many eyes in Abia's direction, a rumour circulated among certain camp participants that she had fatally poisoned three correctors who'd gathered to drink—the kind of act that would draw a fate worse than death on anyone even suspected of culpability. But no one felt they really knew her, not even her close comrades, and no one could verify the rumour.

What was certain was that Abia was respected among her peers and a little feared. She retained this status in Riverwish, where she partnered with a prominent militant soon after her arrival, before suddenly dropping him and withdrawing, for the most part, from militant circles. She's tight-lipped about what happened, but the tone with which she and Sarone speak of those events suggests to Shael that the man may have been violent towards her. (Though Shael has no evidence for this intuition and hasn't asked Abia to confirm it, the face they instinctively picture is Natum's.) Then Abia was alone again, living quietly in the west, until she and Sarone started talking and didn't stop.

Although, in its texture and many of its particulars, Abia and Sarone's love is distinct from Shael and Coe's, Shael feels comforted to behold it in part because of the hope it gives them for their own life. That such intimacy is possible here; that it can work, be generative, stable, a source of peace. And though Abia, Sarone, and Potenza have made a kind of island for themselves in the west, though they form a relatively autonomous unit, in their company Shael almost always feels welcomed and supported. The only time a tension creeps into their evening conversations is when Shael mentions they're no longer just thinking about joining the team that will meet Coe's transport, but have resolved to start training for it. Sarone, holding Potenza in her lap, blinks. "My advice? If you're determined to do this? Find someone else from the camp who will train with you." Maliez shrugs. "I will," she says. "If you want." She looks at Shael with simple, candid affection. "I'd be grateful," Shael says.

Sometimes Sarone sleeps late, and Shael takes a long walk with Abia and Potenza in the shade of the ravine. "Why do you mistrust the others so much?" Shael asks on one such morning. "Those not in the west. Calla in particular. Do you feel it's impossible to recover from an upbringing in the mountains?" Potenza's eyes dart from the two adults to the flash of a bird launching from a branch, a trickling stream, the canopy of leaves that shimmers and sways overhead. Abia, watching her, doesn't reply right away. "I think it's difficult," she says eventually. "I think…if you've been told your whole life that you're exceptional, that you're naturally superior and almost everyone else on the planet deserves no better than the miserable, monotonous suffering to which your people have condemned them…I mean, what a horrible toxin in your system, that idea. If it were me, if I'd been raised that way? And somehow managed to refuse it? I wouldn't boast about how liberated I'd become. I'd spend the rest of my life alert to the danger of that toxin reactivating inside me. I'd never be completely sure whether it were gone or just…dormant." She runs her hands through Potenza's hair. The child draws closer to her. "I don't think Calla has those doubts," Abia goes on. "I don't think she worries about how deeply she may be compromised. She has the arrogance of a saviour. She thinks it's her role to free us all. She doesn't see that we need to free ourselves." Sunlight breaks through the trees' cover a few steps ahead of them, illuminating a circle of ground. False significance, a trick of the light, the lit ground the same as the shadowy terrain all around it. "She's tied her fate to ours, though," Shael says, "she's fighting for her own freedom now as well." Abia exhales. "That's true," she says. "But it's not the same. Like I've said, the stakes are different for her. She'd have a relatively easy time if she chose to abandon us." She hesitates. "For all we know, she already has."

The insinuation that Calla might have divided loyalties would bother Shael less if it hadn't already occurred to them. They believe it and don't. What would she have to gain by spying? Smooth re-entry into the mountains? But she speaks of life there with such venom. Convincingly. And her passionate belief in Riverwish as a project—its models of justice, its intransigent refusal of Flint's ways of being, thinking, doing—seems genuine. Yet Shael is aware they can be credulous, discover deceptions later than most would. Coe's instincts would again be helpful here.

Training takes place in a clearing not far from the Betweens' house, a wide expanse bordered by forest. Several dozen comrades show up, all post-pubescent ages and genders represented—Betweens perhaps overrepresented. Much of their training is just simple exercise, building their bodies' stamina and strength: laps around the clearing, push-ups, pull-ups on bars installed for the purpose. In the camp, only participants tasked with physically demanding work are granted permission to train for strength. Now, here, observing the motley assortment of bodies straining to expand their limits, prejudices about who's likely to be fittest are upended. The female elder outruns the young masculine Between; the stooped Between of indeterminate but advanced age, who walks the halls of their house with such slow, deliberate steps, reveals untold reserves of upper body strength, suspending themselves beneath a pull-up bar, placid, for longer than seems plausible.

Shael and Maliez stick together as they train, encourage each other, sometimes playfully compete. Calla watches them, aloof. She's fit, handles most exercises without much visible strain. The sun is intense, the clearing with little shade; they all apply protective cream to their skin before a session begins. Hans sweats, wheezes after exertion. "Soft mountain stock," he quips. But he seems self-conscious about it. Though leadership during training is decentralized at first, comrades taking turns directing exercises, more definite instructors emerge when the group begins to train for combat. Dorota is a clear leader here, Shael notices. They recall what Sarone and Abia have said, on several occasions now, about how influence and authority in Riverwish are entwined with militancy.

"Narrow your stance, both of you," Dorota urges, as Shael squares off against Hans. Shael practises the jabs and feints they've been taught, how to cover their throat, their solar plexus. Surreal to think they might actually have to use these skills, that an occasion could arise when they'd need to hit another person. This possibility feels far more alien to them than the thought that they themselves might be hurt: this they can imagine easily, vividly. They wonder whether striking another person would transform them in some fundamental way, apparent at once to themselves and others. Coe has been in physical fights, but in the camp they're rare. The camp's violence, though all-pervading, is organized. The corporation has a monopoly over it, ruthlessly defended. Strange, Shael thinks, as Hans lands a too-hard blow against their side, winding them for a moment—strange how they're so much more likely to become a victim of violence in the camp, yet in Riverwish violence feels more personal, and this gives it a distinct awfulness, makes it even harder to conceive.

The others training seem not to hesitate over such considerations. When Calla spars with Maliez, for instance, neither holds back. If anything, they fight with a ferocity that exceeds the guidelines they've been given (*focus on technique, the point isn't to hurt each other*). They pepper their hooks with little laughs, as if to convince those watching—or themselves—that they're comradely, at play. But the elbow Calla digs into Maliez's shoulder blade isn't playful. Maliez buckles, gasps. "What are you doing!" Frozen in place, eyes averted, Calla pants. "Sorry," she murmurs. Maliez is still shaking her head when she steps aside with Shael to recover. "Mountain reflexes," she says, loud enough to be overheard. Uneasy, Shael leads her farther away from the others. Maliez has nodded along with Abia's denigrations of the ex-Mountainers for months now: she's well-primed to impute treachery to them. But Shael saw what Calla did. It did look spontaneous, not a planned attempt to wound—but definitely incautious, cavalier.

The guns have two settings. They discharge bursts of electricity, powerful enough to cause serious damage to a human body but seldom fatal, and they fire solid ammunition. Training covers both settings. The targets are empty metal shipping containers pirated from transports, an impress of Flint's name visible on them. As an electric charge hits a container, it knits itself into an avid blue mouth for an instant before it disappears. The solid ammo cuts right through the metal. Impossible to imagine intentionally doing that to a person's body, Shael feels. Yet if they're to join the team retrieving Coe, they must be sure they could fire their weapon if necessary. When they train with guns (the blue bursts of electricity so quiet, the thwack of solid ammo startling), they feel at times as if they're floating above their body, observing a stranger. There's no version of reality, it seems to them, where they could knowingly maim or kill another person and just go on with their life. They feel they'd go mad, or die themselves. Yet they also feel, when they consider the situation in its totality, that probably there's no collective way forward for Riverwish that doesn't involve violence. It will be done to them if they refuse to do it; their refusal will in no way limit the total violence in circulation. Most likely, there's no road to the liberation of the camp that doesn't involve significant bloodshed. Maybe if all the guards were to defect. If the correctors were to see they'd have no chance and surrender, assessors bringing horrified word to the mountains that there could be no hope of regaining control of the camp.

But that would never happen. Every layer of the camp's defences, all the mountains' fists, would heap violence on the rebellion until it were crushed—or proved uncrushable. Even a negotiated peace between the forces of resistance and their erstwhile oppressors would require a prior period of violent confrontation. The firing of guns. How to assimilate this truth without romanticizing it, as Coe can sometimes do? But also without becoming nauseated to the point of lapsing into denial, a pacifism that pretends difficulties will dissolve if they're not looked at—a romance of a different kind.

Shael takes aim. They don't miss. A blue flower unfurls over the container, which rattles, skitters. The ethical problem matters but won't be resolved in the abstract. They need to train so they can protect Coe. They need to be prepared to fire their weapon if someone is endangering them or their comrades. That much is clear. If they're asked to do violence beyond this basic quantum, this principle of love and self-defence, they don't know how they'll answer. But they'll stay alert to the dangers of violence becoming normalized as its own end. This risk unmasks itself in the way the training group gasps with what might be mistaken for pleasure when, in a sparring match, a tall Between's punch connects squarely with a small man's jaw. A chill runs through

Shael as they stand among the others at that moment—not because they don't at all share or understand the group's reaction, but because they do. They must be careful.

The tone Abia and Sarone take towards them changes, becomes subtly more formal. The couple gives Shael and Maliez a wider berth. Wary, perhaps, of the atmosphere of combat that the two in training may trail into the house. Potenza treats them the same as ever, but she's noticed how her caregivers' behaviour has shifted. "They're scared," she says one day, when Shael and Maliez are briefly alone with her in the house. "They think you won't be their friends anymore, you'll stay with the fighting people. But I know you'll still be our friends." Maliez strokes her hair. "Of course we will. We're not going anywhere." Of this Shael feels less sure. Intercepts of transports keep failing. The risks of every foray feel serious enough that people serving on combat teams are urged to make alternative provisions for any comrades who depend on them for care. "I hope you know how grateful I am for your kindness," Shael tells their hosts a few days before Coe is scheduled to be brought out. "We look out for each other," Sarone says. "No one else is going to if we don't."

The evening before the foray, its small expeditionary team gathers on the roof of the tallest intact building in Riverwish, a seat of business or government or both in earlier times. The team consists of Shael and Maliez, Calla and Hans, Alodia and Dorota. Thick connections between them, layered intimacies—it both comforts Shael and makes them anxious. It's also no accident: as much as possible, foray teams are composed of trained volunteers who have existing relationships of trust. From the rooftop, much of Riverwish can be seen. The flatlands of the west, the town dotted with grey ruins and webbed with green, the broad sweep of forest to the north and east.

"We have a custom here," says Dorota.

The song is in a language unknown to Shael. A melody that's melancholy at first, resolving into sweetness in its final notes. Simple, recursive. Shael picks up the lyrics, joins in with the others. Though they all sing as one, Dorota's crisp voice forms the centre of the sound. When they conclude, she turns to Shael and Maliez.

"Maybe you'd not heard that before. We sing it for many purposes, to come together. The lyric that repeats isn't always directly related to the occasion. Its literal translation is: *Perhaps one day the oceans will forgive us.*"

THE FOREST IS A BLUR OF GREEN AND BROWN beyond the eyes of the speeding spider. Six passengers sit in the Explorer's inner chamber, on plush seats, three to a row: Shael, Calla, and Hans at the front, Maliez, Dorota, and Alodia behind them. One of two such arachnoid vehicles in the settlement's possession, it was captured from Mountainers on a long-ago foray. Its interior strikes Shael as a marvel of sophistication: the front console a network of display panels, the inner chamber all sleek steel, whirring air purifiers, reinforced windows on every side except the rear. How different this journey is compared to their voyage out of the camp, cramped under children's toy boxes in a lightless transport hold. Shael isn't driving, Hans has the most experience with the spider's controls, but they feel they could if they had to. They feel powerful, joyful. They want to absorb every moment, each sight: wild curlicues of birds that explode into the sky as the spider hurtles past them; corridors where the forest abates to reveal a clearing, a half-parched lake; a sudden burst of rain they drive into and, just as quickly, pass out of, as if they'd entered and exited another country, its borders administered by clouds. Their feeling of camaraderie with the others swells. In the cool quiet, it's as if the tensions within the group have dissipated, or at least been suspended: Calla and Maliez address each other amicably, Hans makes no cutting remarks to anyone, and all treat Shael with a particular tenderness. They all realize, maybe, that this journey has an extra layer of urgency for Shael. But Coe's on his way now, Hans assures them. And so are they.

When cradled at a certain angle, the gun slung over Shael's shoulder feels almost weightless. A slight shift in position and it becomes impossibly heavy. They wonder again whether they could fire it at someone. More and more they believe they could, if necessary. As the forest tapers to sparse bushes around them, Shael feels a wave of pleasure at how their body has shed its intuitions of its own powerlessness—the way it felt all the time in the camp. They reach into the satchel at their side, retrieve and swallow an endo. Once, not long ago, their body felt like primarily a site of humiliation and suffering, from which some intense pleasures could be extracted as consolation. Now it feels just as mortal, but far less small. Not because they're holding a weapon, but because they feel capable of fighting, with a variety of instruments and tactics, for their own survival. Because for the first time in their life, it feels conceivable that they might fight and win.

By the time they leave the forest behind them, reach the plains that Shael recalls from the last waking moments of their escape from the camp, they've been travelling for hours. The sun is high, the sky hazy. On the horizon, shimmering but unmistakable: peaks. A grey wall, dust-veiled, seems to climb to the height of the clouds.

Shael glances at Calla. At Hans. "Are those…?"

Calla nods. "They're farther than they look. But not far. We're closer to the mountains than to Riverwish now."

Closer to the camp, too, than to Riverwish? Shael doesn't ask. Instead they grow distracted by dread, their eyes lingering on the mountains' faint shapes in the distance. Such wandering focus feels dangerous, so they try to concentrate on the sun-baked plains in front of them. They press their sunglasses, dislodged by sweat, against the bridge of their nose; they watch as Hans adjusts dials on the spider's control console. Technology in Riverwish is so basic, conservation of energy such a priority, that Shael can sometimes forget the degree of technological power Flint has at its disposal, to what uses it puts the minerals that participants haul from the corporation's mines. Or almost forget: even in the calm of Abia's house, they have yet to break their lifelong habit of glancing over their shoulder to locate the nearest watchful black glass dome lodged in a ceiling.

Now static blooms from the Explorer's front panel. Voices.

"…there's a…no, the storm's in the east, it's…"

"…I'm not going to be caught out here in…"

"…but that…but that's your idea then, I'm not the one who's going to tell them we couldn't…"

"Let's wait on more information."

"Are you getting a signal?"

A man and a woman, to judge by their voices. They speak with the accent of the camp. The fragile bravado of guards. Static swallows their conversation, spits out isolated words.

"…we…and slow…where…we wait?…"

Hans glances at the terrain in front of him. He twists a dial.

"…a shelter due ahead. If the storm moves closer, direct them there."

"Understood, we'll keep a watch."

Deep voices, probably men. With crisper enunciation than the previous ones.

"We're not far from them," Hans says. "They're tracking a dust storm, sounds like. As you heard, there are shelters along the main route, one nearby. They may have reinforcements at the shelter, sentries with weapons, so we should try to reach the vehicle before it gets there. Or after it sets off again, if the storm arrives too soon."

"Won't the storm be in our favour?" Alodia asks. "It would give us cover."

"Chaos won't be in our favour," Dorota says.

"Yes, we want to be able to see what we're doing," Hans says. "We don't want to hit our own in the crossfire."

Shael shivers. The sky's haze seems suddenly more menacing. "We're not far from them now?"

"Not far," Hans confirms, glancing at a panel of the console where a few white dots glow in a grey field latticed with darker grid lines.

The plan is to fire on the camp's vehicle from behind, aiming well below the hold where Coe is hidden. Next, the three comrades now seated in the spider's back row are to jump out and prepare to break into the hold, while Hans accelerates to intercept the camp's vehicle, ramming and immobilizing it if necessary, under covering fire from Calla and Shael if the guards attempt to defend their cargo. Generally they don't. Even when the guards in question haven't been turned, as the ones piloting Coe's transport supposedly have—even when the attack on a transport is genuine, not just a ploy to give collaborating guards plausible cover for their loss of a shipment—most guards see no reason to risk their lives to protect some goods. But during the recent ambushes, comrades have been fired on even as they began what they thought were discreet approaches. Have been met with manoeuvres too sophisticated—too deadly—to be guided by ordinary camp guards. Hence the increased combat training for any comrades participating in forays. And the increased certainty in Riverwish that there must be a spy among them.

The camp's vehicle appears on the horizon, shimmering, sooner than Shael expects. They grip their weapon, release it, fold their sweaty hands in their lap. They glance around the spider's interior at the others, who look tense but focused. Alodia runs their teeth along their lower lip. Dorota is impassive, Maliez perhaps the most visibly concerned. All but vibrating with restless energy, Calla looks at Hans, who's staring straight ahead, jaw set.

"If they dare fire on us," she says, "I promise I won't miss when I fire back."

It takes Shael a moment to understand what exactly they find disturbing about her boast. At first they think they simply dislike the violence. Then they remember—as if they could have forgotten—she's a Mountainer, threatening to rain ammunition on guards who, though oppressors themselves, are also captives in the camp. What did she think when she had her hands on Shael? Was there a note of superior fascination, even disdain, in her desire for them? They swallow hard, focus on the land in front of them, the camp transport, to which they're quickly catching up.

Dust swirls in dense circuits in the sunlight. Shael loses sight of the other transport, the dust casting a spell and disappearing it. When it emerges again, they're almost upon it. Hans adjusts a dial; shards of words crackle through a speaker, mostly indecipherable, pooled in static. He stares at the navigation panel, glances over his shoulder at Dorota.

"What's your opinion? Engage now, or are they too close to reinforcements?"

"They've seen us," Dorota replies right away. "We have to engage, they'll alert their friends now in any case."

Hans tightens his grip on the steering wheel. The spider accelerates. Calla checks her weapon's ammunition chamber. Shael's gaze lingers on the back hatch of the camp transport just in front of them, beyond which is its hold. Coe.

"Are we ready?" Dorota says.

The others murmur affirmation.

"We share serious risks." Alodia, mostly silent till now. "But to be with you here is a pleasure."

"A pleasure," echoes Dorota.

"Thank you for risking yourselves for our friend," Maliez says.

"Thanks for having me along," says Shael.

Dust swarms in all of their faces as the spider's side door slides open. Through the doorway, Shael, the best shot in the group, opens fire on the rear of the camp transport. Below the hatch, beneath the hold. Debris scatters. Shael fires a volley into the camp transport's wheels. Brakes squeal as the damaged vehicle skids, slows. Hans cuts the spider's speed. In an instant, as they've rehearsed, Dorota, Alodia, and Maliez are out the door. Dorota lands on her feet; Alodia goes flying but recovers, seems unhurt; Maliez trips, topples, rights herself. Within moments the three are dashing towards the camp transport, which still creeps forward. Hans accelerates the spider, turns it with a sharpness that launches an arc of dirt. Maintaining enough forward momentum to avoid a collision, it careens in front of the other vehicle.

A loud burst of gunfire hits the spider, its side door still open. Calla screams. Hans ducks, wrests the wheel. Gunfire crashes against their vehicle's exterior. When Shael peers up at the windows, they can see nothing but dust. The spider jerks to the right and the camp vehicle swings into view again. A tall, broad person in a corrector's square-cut black uniform stands, gun at the ready, in an open side doorway. That doorway passes the equivalent opening in the spider. If Shael doesn't lift their weapon and fire immediately, they'll be shot. They may be shot anyway. They lift their weapon and fire.

The inside of the spider is a chaos of dust. Shael coughs, doubles over. Their whole body aches. Covering his mouth with a sleeve of his robe, Hans is still crouched by the controls, piloting on what can't be much more than instinct. Where is Calla? Did she leap from the vehicle? Shael scrambles, searching for her. They can hardly see their own hand extended in front of their face. *Where is Calla?*

A moan rises from just behind them. They're aware, as they bend towards the sound, that the spider is slowing, drifting to a stop. The moan redoubles, lapses into a sob. At first glance they think the blood is dust, red earth pillowing her. Then they wonder how there can be so much of it. How she can still be alive when she's lost so much of it. Her eyes are wide. If she dies for Riverwish, if she's martyred here, will Abia and the others still doubt her loyalty? If she bleeds out on the floor of this dust-choked tool of war stolen from her father's corporation, will they still smear her as a pretender, even a spy? As Shael watches her now, they feel a hot surge of indignation on her behalf. And guilt.

They sit beside her, hold her hand. They're aware, remotely, of Hans clambering out of the vehicle, reports of gunfire nearby, now a bit farther away, now near again. They ask her with their eyes if she wants them to stay with her. With her eyes she says yes. When the others return to the spider, Shael senses before they see that Coe is there. A familiar warmth, lowering itself beside them. A hand on their back.

Coe looks five years older; he looks unchanged. He's unshaven, maybe thinner than he was. His hair is cropped even shorter than usual. As if they had never been separated, as if the pause in their togetherness has been no more than an hour, perhaps a dream, he says: "Under difficult conditions. But to be with you here is a pleasure."

How can he know the idiom of the settlement when he's not yet been there? How does Coe always manifest freedom in advance?

"We'll take care of you," he says to Calla. Shael believes him, is comforted. They watch as he wraps a cloth compress around her leg, applies pressure.

The others are all there. The vehicles' motors are loud, as is the howl of the wind, the ricocheting dust. But there's no other sound. No voices from outside. Alodia has a long gash across one of their forearms. Maliez is covered in dirt, as is Dorota, but both seem intact. Hans climbs back into his seat and sets the spider in motion. As the vehicle crawls forward, Shael can see, through the still-open side door, a motionless body in a black corrector's uniform, sprawled on the earth. In an instant the body is engulfed in dust, disappears. Hans presses a button and the side door slides shut. A fan ejects dust from the interior, not fast enough.

Shael sits with Calla. She coughs. Her eyelids droop, closing for a moment before she forces them back open. Coe wraps another layer of cloth around her compress, pulls it tighter.

"She needs care now," Shael says. Their words feel weak to them, useless. The infirmary in Riverwish is hours away.

"She won't die," Hans says, with weirdly jocular confidence. "Don't worry. We won't allow her to."

She makes no sound. The rest of them stare at Hans. With an air of distraction, he ignores them, keeps driving. The dust is a living wall, undulating against the front screen. They're enveloped by it. An ancient animal, every limb a face. When it abruptly parts, they've left the plains behind them. Their spider rolls over foothills. In front of them the mountains loom.

THE ROOM IS SPOTLESS. ITS SURFACES SHINE IN LOW
light from an unseen source. From the ceiling, maybe; on close observation, it appears to glow. All the room's surfaces are white, or pale—in
the dimness it's hard to discern colour. Its furnishings are sparse and
sleek: the long bed Shael finds themselves on, a column of drawers set
into one wall, a small table and chairs made of translucent plastic. The
pillow beneath Shael's head is incredibly soft. It absorbs them.

They drift. Their mind roves over shifting territory: the camp;
Riverwish; the plains obscured by an angry cloud of dust; that storm
abating at last to reveal the mountains, rising like deformed grey teeth.
The winding path that their spider climbed up the mountain slope,
metal mesh fences on one side of them, on the other side just sky. The
turnoff Hans took, creeping along a channel not much wider than the
spider, a sharp incline levelling off before the descent into a tunnel.
Pitch black apart from the spider's lights, but Hans knew where they
were going. Calla's steady moans—agonizing to hear, but proof that
she was still with them. They emerged into daylight and saw, to their
left, a wall of rock; to their right, a row of enormous airlock domes. The
houses within the domes were mostly hidden from the road the spider
travelled, which was situated well beneath them, but fugitive details
could be glimpsed: a roof ornately tiled in red and brown; a stone tower
with a window of pale blue glass. When, dozing, Shael revisits this

moment of the journey, they imagine a person standing behind that window, visible in silhouette. The window opens from its centre, halves parting. Unhurt, Calla waves.

They drift, and sometimes when they wake they're not alone. Coe sits on the bed beside them, runs his hand along their forehead.

"I'm so exhausted," they hear themselves say.

"Understandable. Rest."

Is it still the day of their arrival? Maybe the reason they feel so disoriented is that they're in the mountains—they, Shael Potenza-brood 9872A—which is impossible. Or maybe because they shot the guard, the corrector, their would-be assailant in the camp transport. Can it still be that same day? How long can one day last?

Their mind goes dark, mercifully, their sleep free of dreams, and while the windowless room looks no different when they wake again, they sense it may be morning. They need to pee. Stumbling from bed, noticing they're no longer in their robe, they remember the set of clean clothes they were handed the previous evening: soft, loose pants and a light-coloured, tapering shirt that flows past their waist. Handed by whom? An elder who lives here. Her name is Martina. They really must pee.

Never have they seen a room for it that's so clean. The ceiling glows with warm light. One wall is a floor-to-ceiling mirror. The toilet is a pristine white, nothing at all like the sheds and squat latrines in Riverwish, the waste holes of the camp. A sink is set into a marble countertop, where several liquid soaps are collected. It's all so simple—and overwhelming. When Shael has read about such cleanliness and order, it's always struck them as fantastical, a romantic projection by people who, in their own lives, knew only squalor. Yet here it is. Here they are.

A long, shadowy hallway leads into an open room drenched in light, where Hans, Dorota, and Maliez recline on broad couches, plates of food in front of them. The light streams through a high wall of windows. The view beyond them makes Shael's heart pound. Airlock domes dot the mountainside as it descends to the plains, which ebb out towards the horizon before transitioning to green, the start of the forest. When

Shael looks far to the southwest, they wonder whether they can see the faintest, thinnest sliver of blue. Land's edge. *The unreachable, the impossible.* But no doubt they're imagining it.

The other half of the room is a kitchen, where Martina is preparing food. Coe and Alodia help, stirring pots and arranging plates alongside her. Shael remembers their first glimpse of her yesterday. The spider approached the house's airlock dome, waited as the dome's first seal retracted with a hiss to let them in. They entered the purification chamber and lingered there. When finally they emerged onto the lawn within the dome—vivid green grass, bright flowers, an astoundingly tall tree—Martina was waiting for them. After the chaos of the plains, the sight of her, with her easy smile and elegant red dress, felt like a Sanem vision. The vast house behind her, its stone quarried from the mountains by earlier generations of participants, Hans told them. The moment's calm soon shaken by the rush to get a medic to Calla, decide whether she was safe to move. Coe's hand on their back, leading them into the house.

"Unfortunately a lot of our food here will be hard on your stomach," Martina says, "but we've made a chili with ingredients you're used to. You should eat—you passed out before taking any food last night."

The chili is familiar to Shael, but they can hardly see it, much less taste it. All they can see is the view. This, too, the corporation had stolen from them until now. Stray ghosts of dust speckle the sky's blue, wheel across it. Sunlight glints off a high point on the airlock dome enclosing the house. A bird descends to the dome's surface and perches for a moment. Perhaps finding the material too hot, it takes off again.

"Been a while since you've had such a full house, hasn't it," Hans says to Martina.

She smiles. "Too long. The quiet is very noisy when I'm here by myself."

"You used to find the noisiness noisy too," Hans says, laughing.

Maybe they were lovers once, or married, Shael thinks, watching Martina join Hans on a couch, Coe and Alodia trailing behind her with plates of food. The two of them share an ease, an affection that seems to testify to long familiarity. Shael has never seen Hans so unguarded, without his habitual defensive irony. Coe watches Hans and Martina intently also. But that's how Coe is watching everything. His eyes remain in constant motion, almost frenetic. Scanning the room, the terrain beyond the windows. Vigilant.

"This is delicious," Alodia says. "Thanks for your hospitality. I'm pretty sick of the rations down there, to tell you the truth."

"Better those rations in our own control than the starvation portions of the camp," Maliez says.

"Where's Calla?" Shael asks. "How is she?"

The silence that falls sends ice through them.

"She'll recover," Martina says quickly. "She'll be...mostly fine."

"She's being philosophical about it," Hans says. "She knew the risks."

"She may not be able to return to Riverwish for a while," Dorota says. "She's struggling bitterly with that."

"If she needs the supports available here," Coe says, "and she has the liberty to stay here, then she should stay."

"I would stay here too, if I could," says Alodia. "Look at this place."

Shael feels stung by a vague embarrassment. What must Coe think of a comrade so easily seduced by comforts?

But Coe surprises them. "One day we'll all stay here," he says. "One day we'll fill this place with life. And if not everyone can live here, then everyone will be able to visit." He gestures towards the windows. "These sights belong to all of us."

"Hear that?" Hans says, grinning, to Martina. "More company for you."

"Your father would've hated it," she says, with an ironic curl Shael has heard before. "But you've always liked what he hated."

Are they siblings? Childhood friends?

"I don't trust many people, you know," Hans says. "But I still believe my own mother is on my side. Call me sentimental."

How is it possible? Though the lines of her face are deep, her posture slightly stooped, she looks not much older than Hans himself.

"The elements are gentler to us here," she says, anticipating Shael's question, maybe reading it on their face. "And we have whole teams of specialists who study how to postpone our physical decay."

"Vampires," says Maliez, sending Shael's mind back to old tales they'd read as a child, courtesy of the camp's licensed library cart. The word was a blurt, and Maliez looks abashed. "I'm sorry…I don't blame you in particular."

"We are vampires," Martina says. "And it isn't just evil, it's also wasteful. So many years stolen from you people and we don't even keep them. We can't. There are only so many years we can use before we die, same as everyone."

"You haven't found a way to live forever?" Alodia asks. It's unclear whether they're serious.

"Human life has been extended a great deal in these parts," Hans says. "But there's a limit."

"That escape from mortality you're talking about…it concerns death by so-called natural causes," Coe says. "It doesn't account for the possibility that the people you think you've crushed might eventually pay you a visit."

They've heard Coe speak this way before, but it still jars them. And it seems off-key as they sit in the home of someone who's offered them refuge.

"This house isn't under surveillance?" Coe asks. "How can it not be?"

"No one visits me uninvited," Martina says coolly. "And no one interferes with my visitors."

"They're one of the old families," Dorota says, her gaze on the windows, the mountain slope. "We owe a great deal to their support."

"I never wanted to be drawn into any of this," says Martina. "But you don't control the direction your children take. And you support your children. In whatever way they choose to pursue their perfection."

Strange to sit with Coe, to be again with Coe. The way he glances at them, speaks to them as if little time has passed since they last saw each other. A pretense, of course. A way of suspending, till they have the privacy to address it, the crucial question: what are they to each other now? Shael is still drawn to him, stirred by the taut grace of his physicality, the delicacy of his face. Yet it's difficult to imagine their sex, and so their relationship, resuming just as it was. Their sex and their relationship were of the camp. The camp's constraints shaped intimate content and form, the fantasies the lovers shared as much as the frequency with which they could steal away to meet. Shael knew about Coe's work with the Blood Moon but wasn't fully incorporated into it, wasn't then a comrade in the sense given to that word in Riverwish: an active companion in struggle. All different now. And for several seasons, Shael has known a freedom, more than inward, that Coe has yet to taste. They wonder whether or how it's marked them. Whether it's transformed them in ways that might affect an old lover's desire for them, or theirs for him.

Yet they still respond to his touch in the old ways, still feel a tumult in their stomach when Coe runs his hand through their hair as the two of them explore a warren of stately hallways. The ceilings glow as they pass. Intricate mouldings line the halls, where the walls display painted portraits, many of whose subjects resemble Hans or Martina. Shael lingers before a painting that seems to depict Hans as a boy, or a relative who bears a strong resemblance to him. The boy, no older than ten, his thin blond hair falling over tidy, symmetrical features, stands in what appears to be a large room full of books, towering shelves of them. He glares at the viewer, at the painter. Someone has forced him to be there, to stand for hours. He would rather be anywhere else.

The grass behind the house is a green so intense it seems unreal. Flower beds ring the yard, line it with blooms of purple, scarlet; sprinklers spring to life, showering the earth as if the water available has no limits. No sooner does Shael think *Daekin would love this* than they feel a flush spread in their cheeks. The airlock dome rises, enormous, from the edge of the yard. Just before it is an elevated platform accessed by a short staircase, a sort of lookout point, with long, pillowed benches and trellises webbed with leaves. Settling there with Coe, Shael notices that the other airlock domes dotting the mountain's slope can be seen but mostly not seen through: the farther away they are, the more opaque they appear. By design? Or a trick of the light? The view of the plains is veiled by dust and haze.

"If you'd built this," Coe says. "If you'd been part of the generation that built this, had been allowed to leave the camp to do this work, wouldn't you have gone mad? To have seen with your own eyes the beauty of this life you were forced to make for others?" He glances at Martina's house, its magnificent masonry, the fine windows of coloured glass gleaming on each of its three floors.

Shael says nothing. They share Coe's anger, but right now they can't feel it. All they can feel is his proximity.

"I trust none of them," he says. "Not our hosts. Not the girl who was shot. They all still benefit from the torture of our relations."

"Hans and Calla…they live in Riverwish," Shael says softly. "I don't always trust them either, but…they walked away from this comfort."

"Did they? Then why are we here? How are we safe here?" Coe stares at the house. "If they wanted to stand with us, they could make it so they'd never be able to return to this place. Destroy an airlock dome. Sabotage the spiders. Do enough damage that they'd be killed on sight if they were to reappear. If they keep choosing to live between two worlds, they're actually choosing this one."

In the camp, in their private corner of the abandoned infirmary wing, this kind of talk would overawe Shael; they would be silent in the face of its grim certitudes. But now they say: "It's not so simple. Their links to the mountains help supply Riverwish. We'd be far more isolated without them. And more dependent on Magent."

Coe's eyebrows lift. At first Shael thinks he may be unaware of Magent's role in sustaining Riverwish, but he doesn't ask about it. Perhaps he's just surprised by how much Shael knows.

"Anyway," Shael goes on, "there are plenty of others in the settlement who think like you. You'll feel at home in the west, where I stay."

The possibility of the two of them living in the same place, without elaborate barriers to visiting each other, without fear of surveillance cameras or guards, ghosts across the space between them. Shael tips their head to one side, eyes wide, an inquisitive animal. Coe wraps a hand around the back of their neck, kneads it.

"You must have been distracted while we were apart," Shael says, their voice light, melodic. "Busy surviving. I hear it was harder, they were crueller to you. I'm sure you didn't have much time to think of me."

They aren't certain how much they're teasing and how much their angst is real, but then Coe is kissing them and it doesn't matter. Do his kisses feel different in the mountains? Hard to say, more data needed. Does the firmness with which he grips their body feel more inflected with desperation now, or less? Is that firmness less or more a roughness? Impossible to tell, they must keep testing, but good to know the questions, helpful to hold the questions at the front of their mind, so that with each touch they can remain curious, with each caress seek knowledge, with each brush of Coe's hand across their clit they can reflect again on whether or how their relationship has been transformed.

They kiss for what feels like a few minutes, might be hours. Maybe they're observed from the house or elsewhere. Shael doesn't care. They feel their body through Coe's hands and realize it's filthy, they haven't bathed since their foray in the howling dust. The image of the official in the camp transport, how that person's body crumpled after Shael fired, settles behind their eyes as Coe grips their bottom through their thin pants, works his hand between the cheeks. Shael freezes, their heart races, sweat pours out of them. But they regain composure fast enough that Coe doesn't seem to notice the disturbance. "What if…" they murmur into his shoulder, their voice unsteady. "What if…I'm not what I was, and now…I'm not what you want?"

Coe works his hand in deeper, runs his free fingers through the curls at the back of Shael's head. He bites their neck, almost gently. "I don't think we have that problem." And it's true that their bodies remember each other, still seem to need each other. That familiar compulsion carries them into the house again, to the room where Coe slept—much like Shael's, though the bed is wider, the ceiling's glow a little warmer, a window of pink glass inviting a beam of roseate daylight inside. Coe presses Shael against the wall, manoeuvres them onto the bed. They've missed his force and their body's reply to it, this sensation of totally letting go. They trust Coe. They still trust Coe. But as he shoves two of his fingers into their mouth, works them in and out—an act Shael normally likes—his aggression has a quality that feels new, and troubling. He seems remote, his force less personal, as if it were itself the point. Whereas his force was once a tactic by which Shael's vulnerability was cracked open, a means of entry into tender layers not only of their body. It made Shael more visible to him, and to themselves. Now, as he flips them onto their front, starts sliding their pants down over their hips, it's as if he doesn't see them at all. Not as *them*. Even with their face pressed into the bed, Shael can sense it.

"Wait," they say. "I'm not..."

Coe keeps yanking down their pants. And while that *Wait...I'm not...* is the kind of protest Shael would habitually squeak (albeit in a different tone) as part of their agreed-upon scenes in the abandoned infirmary wing, while they haven't said *overwhelmed*, the code word they set long ago to signal an immediate desire to stop, Coe still seems to keep tugging at their pants for longer than he should.

"Coe!"

He jolts as if snapped out of a trance. "Yes?"

It's not as though Coe doesn't take small liberties sometimes. Not as though he always asks permission in words, aloud. But the way he treads those lines feels more tolerable, safer, when he seems also to dote on Shael. Now they feel like he's using their body as an outlet. A sponge to absorb his excess rage.

"Did I do something wrong?" he asks.

He didn't. Not really. And now that he's stopped, Shael feels they've overreacted. He did nothing terrible. He put his fingers in their mouth and started to pull down their pants. So he hesitated a moment before stopping. Then he stopped.

"Could we just...it's been a while..."

"Yeah." He sounds uneasy, rattled, though not impatient. "We don't have to."

Shael doesn't meet his gaze. "I've thought about it all the time. About you." They feel their eyelids flutter involuntarily. "Nobody else corrects me so well."

Coe's grin is tentative. "Sounds like you're overdue."

"You're going to correct me here?"

"You deserve it here as much as anywhere."

Their clit twitches. They lean towards Coe, kiss him. He places a hand between their legs, strokes them. They gasp.

"Do you need to be punished? Or have you shed your habit of disobedience now that you're free?"

"You don't have a correction paddle here."

"I have my hands."

"Not strong enough," Shael says, and immediately they feel a thrill as Coe's eyes flash, and they jump out of the way, but Coe is too fast for them, both of them know it, and he grabs them and flips them over. Now their pants come down in one pull.

It hurts. When Coe smacks their bottom with only his hand, swinging hard from the start, it burns so much that sobs rise in them almost at once. Coe scolds them. "You." *Smack.* "Do not." *Smack.* "Tell me." *Smack.* "My hand isn't." *Smack.* "Strong enough to correct you." *Smack smack smack.* "Or I'll correct that opinion." He delivers his hardest stroke yet. Shael howls. They're so turned on that they feel they might come into the bed their clit is pressed against. It isn't that they forget how they felt just moments earlier—the danger, the impersonality of Coe's aggression. But now they feel the need to be corrected, to be touched this way, more than they need to be assured of their safety. They also no longer experience what Coe's doing to them as impersonal. *They* are the one Coe is correcting. *They* are the one whose tears Coe's drawn.

They have no barriers with them, but Shael has been taking Melomtin, the drug that allows Mountainers to "pursue their sexual perfection" without fear of pregnancy or most infections, and with which Riverwish is well-supplied. Coe seems startled when Shael, panting on their stomach, reaches back and removes Coe's fingers and guides his cock towards them. They explain, succinctly, and—working together, with care and spit—slide Coe in. They have so missed this. His hands reach around and cup their breasts. They have missed this so much.

"Are you going to be good for me?" Coe says, his voice soft. Shael moans. "When I take you home. To our new home. Are you going to behave and do as I say?"

"Yes."

"If you don't. You know what I'll do."

"You'll correct me."

"I'll send you back to the camp."

They reach behind them and grab Coe's balls. They hiss, without a hint of play: "You'd have to kill me first."

He hesitates, then strokes their hair, suddenly gentle, drawing their curls behind their ears.

"You're right. If we ever go back to the camp, we go together. To liberate it."

They won't deny the violence in him, or romanticize it. But they also can't deny that it's entangled with parts of him they love, sides of him that give them pleasure. Give them hope.

Afterwards, they lie naked together in the perfect quiet of the house. Nowhere else has Shael seen anything like the light that streams through the pink window, its pale enchantment. Maybe the light in the Betweens' house, in the second-storey bedroom where they've passed languid hours with Alodia, comes close.

Running their fingers down the far side of Coe's torso, it takes Shael a moment to register what they're feeling, the ridge that wasn't there before, shouldn't be there. They lift their head to look. The scar is huge, running from Coe's armpit nearly to his pelvis.

"From the day we tried to get out of the camp together?" Shael murmurs.

Coe nods. "I'd never have left you on your own if I'd had a choice."

The loss he must've felt, to have been taken back inside Flint's walls while Shael and Maliez stayed free. And the shame, maybe—as if he were abandoning the others.

Shael burrows their face into Coe's chest, studies the valley of his hips. "I shot someone," they say. "A corrector, or a person dressed like one. In your transport. I think I killed them."

Coe runs his fingers through Shael's hair. "They would've killed you if you hadn't."

"Maybe."

"Certainly."

"How do we keep from becoming...the same as them? I know if I fire a weapon to defend myself I don't turn into a torturer, but..."

"No *but*. Fighting to free ourselves and those we love isn't the same as what they do to us. At all."

Shael agrees. In the abstract. But they're haunted by the gaze of the Flint official they shot. Sunglasses jarred off in the tumult, eyes flashing wide, stunned. In their last moments of sight, of life. "You've killed, then?"

"Yes," Coe says.

"How did you cope?"

He's silent for long enough that Shael becomes anxious, glances up at his face. His expression is flat. At last he says: "Do you know how many times they've beaten me? Not in a fun way. Beaten me so horribly I thought I might die. And how many of my kin they've brutalized or murdered? As if it were nothing? As if we were just factors of production for the executives to manage? We have an obligation to end this evil by any means necessary."

"And if the means are also evil?"

"If you hadn't shot that person, they would've shot you."

"It's not only..."

They're thinking of the council chamber, the threat of a Second Process lurking behind the apparent compassion of a trial's proceedings.

"Try to be realistic," Coe says. "Sentimentality will get us nowhere."

"I don't want to risk my life to make a world as vicious as the one we've left."

"You'd risk your life by *not* acting as well. It's just a question of who you decide to stand with."

"I stand with you. But we, I mean all of us…we need to talk about these things."

"I never said we didn't."

Yet Coe has no experience of public deliberative processes, the kind of forums Riverwish has established. The thinking and planning he's done with like-minded others has always been furtive, aspirations to thoroughness and democratic fairness subordinated to the need to be quick, speak obliquely, not get caught.

"But we protect each other," he goes on. "No matter what. I'll protect you."

"I want to protect you too."

"You do. You did. You fired."

Still uneasy, Shael kisses him to change the subject.

Hours pass before their growling stomachs lead them downstairs again. They find all the others, except Calla, in the room with the sweeping view. But now a curtain has been lowered over the windows, and an image of a vast library is projected on a wall.

"The jewel of the mountains," Hans says. "They expended more work hours and human suffering on constructing the library than on nearly any other single project."

Its bookshelves are arranged in rings that seem to ebb outward without end. Floors and floors of them. A round glass column, in which a shining silver elevator can be seen, rises through the rings' centre. A golden glow appears to suffuse the entirety of the library, more than bright enough to read by, but not harsh. The next projected image reveals, on the library's highest floor, an observatory with a transparent dome, Mountainers at leisure there. Flaxen-haired children, adults with symmetrical features, tall and athletic. Stars twinkle in the night sky glimpsed through the dome. Another projected image reveals the view down the mountainside from the edge of the observatory, at twilight: a cascade of airlock domes built into the rock, white and gold lights glimmering within; outside the domes, the black openings of tunnels like sightless eyes; crawling between them, two steel spiders, a green light shining from each of their backs.

"We'd love to take you to all these places," Martina says. "But it's not safe for you."

"Or for us," Hans adds.

More images appear on the wall, each perfumed with the saccharine self-satisfaction of Flint's celebration-day films. Why was this photo series assembled, Shael wonders. To demonstrate Flint's virtues to the other corporations in the world system, in competition for prestige? Or just to stoke Mountainers' own pride at what they'd built? A sprawling park, sealed under airlock. An assembly of smiling children in front of a long stone building, all wearing identical uniforms, maroon with black trim. It takes Shael a moment before they realize where they've seen those uniforms before. Potenza, their mother, used to fabricate them. She would bring them home to the dwelling hub if she hadn't completed her quota during the workday. They were so small that Shael always figured they were meant for other children. These children. Many of whom resemble Calla enough that they could be her kin.

Shael doesn't want to look at these images anymore.

"Where's Calla? Can she have visitors now?"

She's recovering in a bedroom on the third floor that looks just like the others, except with a broader window, now curtained, and medical supplies spread on a bedside table: boxes of pills, a stack of clean bandages, a wide roll of gauze. In bed, under a thick blanket, she's reading a book, its cover brown and hard-backed and blank.

"This was removed from the library." She sounds a bit raspy, but also playful, alert. "Lucky that Martina has a copy. An old favourite. I've read it many times. It tells the story of a prisoner insurrection that seizes the camp and eventually threatens the executives where they live. Here. The author was popular enough, from an important enough family, that she could publish this and not attract too much trouble at first. But people got nervous. It's a rare text now. You can read it if you'd like. *Blood and Moonlight.*"

Shael blinks. The Blood Moon. "Who was the author?" ·

"A woman named Miriam Lefebvre. She lives near here, quietly."

"She's…a friend of ours."

"Yes."

"But the book is fiction."

"For now."

She tries to sit up a little, winces. Her eyes, when they meet Shael's, seem to apologize for her frailty. But they're as bright as ever.

"They say you might stay here."

"I really don't want to. But…"

Her gaze rests on her lower body.

"I could show you, but it's…a bit startling."

They feel suddenly cold again.

She pushes the blanket just a little to one side, away from them. They see nothing out of the ordinary. No. They see…nothing.

"They had to remove it below my knee," she says. "I won't walk again. Not unless I stay here and get fitted for a prosthetic. Which is an option available to me. At a high personal cost."

"It isn't right," Shael whispers, their throat tight.

"I knew the risks. And worse is done all the time to your people in the camp."

Every moment when they wondered whether she could be the spy, the architect of the settlement's recent disasters, now makes them feel nauseous with guilt.

"If it hadn't been this, it could've been a raid," Calla says. "We lead dangerous lives."

"But you didn't have to. You chose to put yourself in danger for our sake. You could've just stayed here and lived comfortably."

"Please. What do you think people do here all day, if they're not tasked with managing the corporation? It's all hobbies and copulation and intrigue. The same faces, the same old inbred families. No new opinions, no real debate, except about trifles. It's evil, but it's also just so *dull*. I won't stay here even now, not if I can help it."

"How will you manage?"

"We take care of each other in Riverwish. Even those who need more care than others. Especially those." Tapping her book, she goes on: "Anyway, I couldn't let you all bring my favourite story to life and leave me out."

They're reminded of the ways Abia and others in the west speak of her: criticisms that she's a comfortable, spoiled person play-acting the role of the revolutionary. But those criticisms are wrong, Shael feels now. Wildly wrong.

"We wouldn't leave you out," Shael says. "You're the one who's read the history of our future."

"Hm, yes. Lefebvre is probably my favourite living author. But I can tell you that the book concludes on an ambiguous note. Open-ended. The history of our future is still unwritten." She sets the book down on the table beside her pills. "You must be happy to see him again."

Shael hesitates just a moment before they nod.

"Be careful," she says. "He's done important work. Helped organize extensively in the camp. We owe him a lot. But his rage hasn't always remained focused on the enemy. You should stay alert."

Everybody is always warning them about everybody else.

"I wonder…" Shael says. "When we write the history of the future, will we be able to record that finally we could trust one another?"

She looks at them with affection, a tenderness that rises from her mouth to her eyes and radiates. "Maybe. Yes. That's the test. That's how we'll know we're free."

SCARS

THE DISTURBANCE IN RIVERWISH IS OBVIOUS AS soon as Shael arrives. Every face in the streets seems downcast. Even the west, placid already, feels deadened. Shael wonders whether there was a raid. Were comrades wounded, killed? Only when they meet Abia at her house do they learn what's happened.

Bradoch, the pianist, found the body. The man had shed so much weight that he may well have been unrecognizable to almost anyone besides the Betweens with whom he'd settled. Certainly he bore little resemblance to the man he'd been not long earlier, who'd stood in the council chamber and, trembling with defiance, called the community a mob. Bradoch and the others had noted his intensifying paranoia, his growing mistrust even of those who'd been his confidants among the Betweens, who'd struggled with him. But they hadn't believed he would end his own life. They'd considered him too proud. When they spoke of it later, they would reflect that his pride may have increased the danger. A less arrogant man might've suffered with more patience the reduction of his status, his horizons. Natum couldn't.

The burial, conducted promptly according to custom, is finished by the time Shael and Coe and the others reach Riverwish. The evening of their return, a memorial ceremony is held in the food hall, attended by nearly as many people as were at the man's trial. Comrades are offered a chance to speak, and a few accept, most of them Natum's relations, offering words about the contradictions of his character and how the loss of even a difficult member of the community is terrible— comments that draw scattered murmurs. But for the most part, the gathering is informal, a chance to catch up, commiserate, gossip. Not unlike a leave-taking ceremony in the camp, Shael thinks, one of the few collective practices of freedom that Flint prisoners would reliably insist on, despite the dangers. A refusal to pass over a death in silence, as if the life lost were no more than a digit on an assessor's balance sheet.

The foray team minus Calla, who has remained in the mountains for now, are all there. They're clustered in a corner of the hall, along with a number of other Betweens. Coe sits just apart from the rest of them, hunched over a cup of tea, stirring it with a finely carved bamboo spoon—unmistakably an item that made its way to Riverwish from the mountains, but to which Coe reacts not at all. Everything needed to be explained to Shael when they first arrived, there was no end to their questions, but Coe greets all the settlement's details as if they're entirely natural to him, expected. Perhaps they are, given the lines of communication that exist between the Blood Moon and this place.

Fragments of nearby conversations pass into Shael's awareness: by all appearances, the spy is the only subject anybody wants to talk about. There are still no definite suspects, so everyone suspects everyone, and also can't bring themselves to believe that anyone they know might be a murderous traitor. Natum's death has rattled a community already on edge. That background tension seems to make the loss feel less staggering to the collective than it otherwise might; even at this memorial ceremony, more comrades can be heard discussing infiltration than the events around Natum. Yet it also feels as though any shock, such as Natum's death, might now be enough to push the tense settlement over the edge, into a spiral of recriminations and rancour that could prove difficult to stop.

"Horrible thing, isn't it."

Shael turns to see Daekin a step away, hands folded neatly in front of them, green eyes bright.

"If you were to include deaths like Natum's in the tally of those condemned in our council chamber, the body count would be much higher."

Shael's breathing is shallow. "It happens often, then."

"Not often. But too often."

A strange privacy envelops their conversation, as if it can't be seen or heard by the many others nearby. And in fact no one appears to be watching them.

"What would you suggest?" Shael asks. "How could the risks be lowered?"

"More clarity and speed, for a start. He was left in limbo. A committee of elders was supposed to meet to recommend next steps for him, but it hadn't yet convened. He was beginning to suspect they would let him drift, abandon him to his internal exile. He felt they might just forget about him and move on. He wasn't wrong to fear it. He'd seen it happen to others. We all have."

"And if they'd moved faster? You believe he would still be alive?"

"Hard to be sure. He'd lost a great deal of what he valued. And there was little chance of him recovering it. Even in the best-case scenario for him, the elders were never going to be able to restore his prestige."

"He might've rebuilt it over time. He was charismatic."

"Maybe," Daekin says. "If he could've been patient. Which seems doubtful, from all I'd seen of him. I'd known Natum for a long time."

They enunciate these words carefully, with a strange control. And Shael recalls what Calla told them of Daekin's ostracism, their historic conflict with the community: how it began when Daekin exposed the manipulations of charismatic men.

"He spoke against you," Shael says. "Back then."

"Yes."

"And still you comforted him after his fall. Struggled with him."

"It was my duty." A playfulness appears in their eyes. "It was also a subtle pleasure. To be kind to those who have arrogantly wielded their influence against you, to be gentle with them when they're brought low."

Shael watches them for a moment. Grows uncomfortable, averts their gaze. "Why did he speak against you?"

"I saw Natum's callousness, his entitlement, the way he treated women and some Betweens as if our bodies were his pay for services rendered to the collective, and I had enough influence myself to be a danger to him, though not enough to protect myself from him. And from others like him—he was far from alone in that behaviour. They started a rumour that I was propositioning women they considered their own, during raids. I wasn't, but two of their intimates backed them up, so I was disbelieved. And, you know, people like us"—their jaw tightens, their eyes cloud for a moment as they glance at Shael— "we're always a little suspect to people like them, it's never hard for them to believe we're engaged in...deviations. So I was isolated. It gave rise to an astonishing rage in me. I went through seasons of it, cycles of wishing for revenge, conciliation, revenge again, and so on. But my most lasting reaction was that as much as it was in my power, I refused to let the same thing happen to anyone else."

Shaken, Shael doesn't know what to say. "I'm sorry."

"It was all a long time ago," Daekin replies, with unconvincing nonchalance. "Decades. A whole generation ago."

"You and Natum were both founders," Shael says, a swirl of chaos in their gut.

Daekin hesitates, blinks. "That's right."

"How did it feel to leave what you'd known? Your kin? For such uncertain prospects out here." A trembling in their lips and jaw as they speak. They wonder whether it's visible.

"Probably about the same as you felt when you left the camp."

"I knew it had been done before. I knew there were others awaiting me here."

"Maybe you would have attempted it even without those reassurances. If you felt you were living the life of a shadow. If you had the power to imagine things might be very different. Which you do, I think."

"If my lover hadn't wanted me to leave with him, and supported me, I'd never have found the courage." Their gaze flickers to Coe, still hunched over his tea.

"The same was true of me."

Shael feels blood rush to their face.

"Desire can be a bridge," Daekin says. "It can enable us to take risks we'd never have considered otherwise. Risks that point far beyond the desire itself. I don't think that's a bad thing."

They hesitate. It seems as if they might say more, but Coe's voice cuts in.

"Let's leave soon," he says. "I don't want to travel in darkness."

"I know the way well," Shael says.

"No doubt. But I'll feel better if I can see what's around us."

His habits of vigilance will take a while to calm here. Maybe they won't calm. Maybe that's fine, will afford them additional protection. "Whatever you prefer."

"Come see me at the house, if you'd like," Daekin says. "I can tell you stories of the early days. You seem to have some archival curiosity."

Shael struggles for words. After a moment, they just murmur thanks.

Night is falling by the time they begin their journey back to the west. It's been agreed that Coe will join Shael's home for now. Earlier in the day, when they travelled there to make introductions, Abia and Sarone greeted Coe with a peculiar blend of wariness and warmth. As they reflect on it, Shael realizes this is more or less how Maliez, too, engaged with Coe when they were reunited. Potenza, on the other hand, embraced him immediately as a new friend. Shael intuits that the house is unlikely to be a long-term dwelling for them and Coe together, but for now, while it lasts, they feel warmed by the thought of sharing space with all these comrades to whom they've grown close. It feels like a broadening and deepening of kin—a consolation, if never a replacement, for the kin they've left behind.

The shadows that have descended over the path to the west are thick enough to make Coe visibly uneasy, his eyes darting. Or perhaps that's just the way he looks now, the way he's long looked: watchful. The houses and ruins in their gated courtyards are ghostly. Coe pauses to peer through a gate, presses against it; it gives way. A glint of amazement in his eyes: *No locks.* If innocents are staggered to discover the evil that people can do, Coe, a creature of the camp, suffers the same shock at the sight of unusual human trust. *How is this possible?* An uncanny mirror image of young Potenza, hearing of the camp. *It's like a dream to her. She can't believe it exists.* The world may let innocence survive in some and strip it from others, Shael thinks, but wonder can also be reclaimed.

The sky is dark by the time they reach the flatness of the west. There are no cyclists visible, and only a few distant lights by which to orient themselves.

"This traitor that everyone speaks of," Coe says. "The spy. Do you suspect anyone in particular?"

His bluntness is jarring.

"I...no," Shael says. "It makes no sense. Nobody here stands to benefit from comrades getting ambushed on forays."

"Are you sure?"

They hesitate.

"You trust the people you live with," Coe goes on.

"Yes."

"But they rely on Magent."

Shael feels a surge of defensiveness. "Just like the rest of Riverwish relies on skimming from Flint."

"By sabotage and theft. Not the same as making a deal with them."

"We make deals with Flint's guards, don't we? The ones who've been turned."

"It's different. They share our risks."

"If we didn't have Magent's people here, Flint would blast us apart."

"Is that what you believe? Or what your friends have told you."

With a faint howl, a gust of wind flutters their robes.

"They're from the camp," Shael says. "They lived like us there. They share our risks, as you say. You'd rather trust the…" They're about to say *hobbyists from the mountains*, before reflecting again that several of those hobbyists helped save Coe's life, and one lost a limb in the process. How much of Abia's thinking have they internalized? "You'd rather trust the people who could return to the mountains whenever they like?"

"I'd rather trust as few people as possible."

"Life here can't function that way. Trust is necessary when we depend on each other so much for everything."

"But does that trust really exist? In practice? Do you see it?"

Shael fixes their gaze on the lights of the next house. "I see people trying to build it."

"It'll take generations." Coe says this flatly, without apparent grief. "A re-education of human character that would support the kind of trust you want? I believe it's possible, I think the people who tell you it can't be done are servants of the camp, whether they know it or not. But we'll never live to see it."

They think again of young Potenza, what's normal for her. "But others will."

Coe doesn't reply.

"Wait till you spend more time outside the camp," Shael goes on. "You might be surprised by how a new environment changes your thinking."

"You and me…the camp didn't treat us the same. We didn't live the same life there. I carry it with me in ways you don't."

"We all do, all of us who—"

"It's *different*," Coe says, with a sharpness close to anger. Almost frightening. "I did what I could to make sure you'd never suffer what I went through," he continues, his voice softer now. "I got you out."

"I'm grateful," Shael murmurs.

"It's just too late for some of us, more than others."

Shael is rattled enough that they don't reply. A comrade deciding it's too late for themselves, that they're irredeemably broken…it feels like a dangerous resignation, an excuse for not even trying to wash the camp from their personality, for making no attempt to purge themselves of uncontrolled, maladaptive violence. *Too late* means no will to grow, means *take me or leave me*. It occurs to Shael that they've never heard a Between declare that anything, for anyone, is too late. Sometimes they even feel the essence of Betweenness is a steadfast conviction that while a person is still living, it's never too late for transformation.

"I think you're good," Shael says quietly. "What the camp did to you…it can be undone. I believe that. The time I've lived here has made me believe it." Not everyone who takes refuge at the Betweens' house remains broken.

For a moment Coe doesn't respond. Then: "You've always thought I'm good." No bravado now, no aggression. His voice is faint. "I don't know why."

"Because it's obvious. It always has been."

He turns his face away from them. What is he afraid they'll see?

"I want to be…the person you think I am," he says, barely audible. "I don't know whether it's possible. But it's what I want."

All the lights are aglow in the house where they're staying. Sarone appears in the doorway with Potenza, silhouettes of welcome. The footsteps of those returning, on the hard earth and amidst no other sounds but the wind, must have been audible from a distance.

"Good evening," says Potenza, with warmth and crisp formality. "To be with you again is a pleasure."

The wind's low moan underscores their conversation as they sit together in the main room. Coe holds one of Abia's wooden sculptures, a dog. He runs his fingers over its smooth surfaces.

"We were taught they were almost extinct," he says. "Only some wild ones remaining in the Waste, spawning sick generations. But it's not true." Potenza stares at him, rapt, eyes wide. "The loyal, gentle kind we read about in texts—they have them in the mountains. All sorts of dogs."

"We have to free them," Potenza whispers with absolute seriousness. The others laugh. Realizing she's said something funny, she giggles. But insists again: "I want them to be free."

"We'll rescue them all," Coe says, a broad smile transforming his face, making him look years younger. How he might've looked all the time, had he been born into a different life. "When we storm the mountains, we'll bring treats. Once the dogs defect, we'll know we've won."

More laughter. Shael feels warmth trace long trails through their body. They could get used to living like this.

The conversation turns to the memorial ceremony for Natum. "Many were there?" Abia asks.

"Lots of people," Shael says.

"Did Caiben attend?" Sarone asks.

"I thought I saw him," Shael says. He looked like a different man. Even from across the hall, he appeared healthier, colour in his cheeks, more substance on his slender frame. He was standing in a large group of others, speaking freely, sometimes smiling. Maybe smiling a bit too much, given the sombre occasion. But it was a relief to see he'd been restored to a secure place in the community.

"The trial process is vicious," Abia says abruptly. "It's an idealism that kills, we've seen this over and over."

"We do need a way of dealing with wrongs," Sarone says. "And a way to uncover the truth about them, first of all. A process. Look how much energy has been expended to try to find the traitor among us. Council meetings, interviews, new security and information-sharing protocols. Dorota interviewing us, sitting with us for hours, all that care and diligence."

"Inviting men to search my workshop, search Potenza's room, yes, I remember very well," Abia says, with a sourness she doesn't bother to hide.

"My point is that you need systems in place for when there are problems," says Sarone. "You can't do such things haphazardly."

Abia shakes her head, as if exhausted by this subject that's swelled to take up so much space in Riverwish's public life. "The spy is an exceptional case, I accept that. But when it's a matter of private conflicts, often the truth is unknowable. Or the collective knows it in advance, without the help of any trial. Everyone knew about Natum."

"Everyone also believed Natum's smears about Caiben."

"Not everyone. Some. And, as usual, time would've vindicated him. The truth would've come out. Caiben isn't dangerous."

"Well, he did strike Natum."

Their debate flows without tension, with a regular cadence, as though they've had this kind of conversation routinely, a motif in their relationship. Potenza glances between her caregivers.

"These matters are difficult when everyone involved has been shaped by the camp," Coe says. He turns to Potenza. "Maybe when you serve in the council chamber, it'll be different."

"I can serve now if I want," she says, not bragging, just stating a rule. "If I choose to. They know I'm small, they'll make allowances for that."

"You have other things to do," Sarone says. "Like arithmetic."

"I can do both," Potenza says.

When they retire to sleep, Coe joins Shael in their bed. Their kisses are lazy, slow. Coe seems to have relaxed. He runs his hands through Shael's hair, wrapping curls around his fingers as if to tighten them.

"Thank you for bringing me here," he says. "And for risking yourself to get me out. You didn't have to. I wouldn't have wanted you to. But thank you."

"To be with you here is a pleasure," Shael murmurs, and takes his cock into their mouth.

Their sleep is thick with dreams. They're with Coe, Coe is leading hundreds of comrades from Riverwish, they're raiding the camp. The guards have all been turned or forced to flee. The camp's gates stand open, and its dwelling hubs' doors. Participants crowd the halls, throng in their thousands. The correctors open fire on them but are swarmed, or surrender and are disarmed. Some of them, the most notorious, are not permitted to surrender. Messages are scrawled across every wall of the camp, all its colour-coded corridors, its workshops, its hard correction centres.

No more cages, no more locks.

Revolutionary love comes armed.

Never again, for anyone.

The symbol of the Blood Moon, an almost-sphere with three wavy lines trailing from its convex side, proliferates everywhere. Participants flood beyond the camp's ring roads and perimeter wall, mass in the scorching sunlight. They're no longer participants; they've become something else. And they are legion. An ocean of them.

It may be the same dream or another in which the mountains are taken. The same dream or another in which an airlock dome reverberates with the yips and barks of a hundred dogs. Brown and gold and black, playful, some wrestling each other but most occupied with those who gather round them: hundreds of children. Not pale children, or not only. The camp's children. Young Potenza is there, transfixed by an enormous, gentle hound. Elders are there as well. Shael spots their mother across the lawn. She looks the same as when they last saw her, but without the usual anxiety that stoops her shoulders, strains her face. Their small siblings, who look the same as when Shael last saw them, laugh among the dogs and other children.

It's Martina's yard. And now Shael is watching it from above, through a window in the house, in a bedroom. Coe is behind them, on the bed, naked. Shael knows this without turning to look. They know without looking that Coe is covered in scars. They lift their gaze from the yard to the airlock dome, the plains beyond it, the forest on the horizon. They're startled to discover that the plains are not empty. A vast darkness inches over the terrain. The army must be thousands strong. Armoured vehicles border the troops. Alongside Martina's airlock dome, dozens of steel spiders descend to the base of the mountains. At first Shael thinks the clash between Flint and Magent has come. But then they glance again at the yard, the dogs and the camp's children and elders at play. And they notice, on each of the spiders, a strange red protrusion. A flag. A moon almost full, three wavy lines trailing behind it. When Shael turns to face Coe, Coe is smiling. Coe is covered with scars. Coe is crying. "You were right," he says. "I never thought I'd live to see it. You believed. I love you. You were right," he keeps repeating, and he doesn't stop until Shael takes him in their arms and quiets him.

SHAEL IS IN THE GARDEN WITH DAEKIN MOST DAYS.
They speak of seeds, generation, how to grow beauty from deathly soil.
There are new trials, sometimes new internal exiles who join them at
the Betweens' house, where Shael is present often enough to be aware
of most goings-on. Alodia has angered a man by speaking openly of his
violence against his partner, is concerned for their own safety. A young
Between named Clarite is denounced for neglecting their child, hardly
more than an infant; both child and parent receive ongoing care at the
house. A man named Leo, one of the defectors from the mountains, is
accused of caressing a woman's lap under the table in the food hall one
night. The woman is a stranger to him, she had not agreed to his touch,
he hadn't sought permission. He denies the claim and a trial is called,
where a dozen other women describe identical experiences with him.
He retreats to the house.

In the garden there are vines that climb a small wooden fence, and
vivid flowers. Leafy shrubs form hedges, afford the garden an atmosphere of privacy, though it's open on most sides. It's in this space of
quiet that Daekin begins to speak one afternoon, unprompted, about
their last days in the camp. How their lover, another Between, active
in the revolutionary group that preceded the Blood Moon, began to
tell them about an experiment some were planning. Conversations
underway with accomplices in the mountains. A jailbreak. A new start.

Daekin spoke of it with their partner, their licensed match, with whom they had a small child. (It's at this point in the story that Shael begins to feel dizzy.) *Matio says they can get us out,* Daekin told her. *Us,* Daekin's partner said. *If we all wish to risk it,* Daekin said. *They love me, they care for you and the child, I trust them.* Their partner believed it could be a trap, an attempt to lure revolutionaries to their deaths. That there might be nothing beyond the camp, the Waste would swallow them. *If it were just me,* she said. *But the child,* she said. *But I couldn't tell you to stay here. In your condition. Knowing the dangers. You must choose for yourself.*

"I agonized over the decision," Daekin says now. "I couldn't bear to leave the child. But in the end there was no way I could justify remaining. I was in danger, and Matio was in danger, and I couldn't protect my partner or our child. I had to take my chances. I promised I would come back for them when I could. Or find a way to get them out."

Shael has stopped moving. They're just standing in the sunlight, staring at Daekin. They had expected that if they ever learned the truth, ever found the courage to ask, the day of revelation would be somehow otherwise auspicious: some inward or outward crisis would force disclosure. But it's a day like any other. The wind whispers through the trees and tall grasses as ever, indifferent. Daekin doesn't turn to face Shael, keeps attending to the soil they're seeding. A long moment passes in this way.

It's Shael who at last breaks the silence. "You heard my name. You knew. You didn't say anything."

Daekin's hands work the earth. "I didn't think I had a right to."

"You just let me wonder."

"I was afraid. I thought you'd hate me."

Shael is trembling. But they don't hate them.

"I wouldn't blame you if you did," Daekin goes on. "But I couldn't bear to find out. I wasn't trying to be cruel. I'm just a coward."

"Runs in the family," Shael says, and Daekin looks at them, eyes clouding with an unspeakable grief.

"But I kept my promise to you," Daekin says, their voice breaking. "I kept my promise."

In a report from the Blood Moon, concerns were raised about one of the militants' lovers, a young Between, how their vulnerability could be exploited to compromise the militant. The Between wasn't named, but Daekin wondered. Hoped. The number of years that had passed. The resemblance the story bore to their own. They suggested that the Between be brought out, if they would come. They advocated this course of action with an uncharacteristic assertiveness. The militant should do what he could to persuade his lover, even if that meant the militant came out as well and so was no longer working for them in the camp.

"Eventually more information emerged and confirmed my hunch," Daekin says. "It took all my restraint not to visit you when you first arrived. But Calla assured me she would bring you here."

It's as if Shael has always known: the fact of Daekin, who Daekin is to them, writes itself in an instant not only on all the future's pages but also on each surface of the past. It's as if they've always been aware that their parent was a Between, a revolutionary, a founder, the gardener in the clearing who prepared the way for them.

"Do you remember my mother?"

"Always."

"Do you miss her?"

"Of course."

"But you let her go."

"She let me go. As she did you."

What is Potenza doing now, the elder Potenza who raised Shael? Who lived her life with perfect outward obedience to the dictates of the corporation, a model participant, sacrificing her body and spirit to labour so she might keep her unusual child safe. Does she still obey, still file into the work halls to weave clothes for the children of the mountains? She must. Though Shael feels it's irrational, a surge of resentment rises in them—not towards her, but towards Daekin.

"Why didn't you get her out too? If you were able to help me do it?"

"She was asked. She has young children now, we were told. We couldn't bring them all out, and she wouldn't leave them behind."

Unsurprising. She would never have left the young ones alone with Tann, a man who couldn't be trusted not to neglect or strike them even when she was there and vigilant. Still it hurts Shael to hear.

"One day we'll free them all," Daekin says. And with a hint of playfulness: "Even the ones we dislike."

"What about the ones we dislike because they do violence? Because they're a danger to others?"

"We struggle with them."

If Daekin weren't their parent, if Shael didn't understand now beyond doubt that Daekin is their parent, maybe they'd be impressed by the elder's dedication to such struggle and leave it at that. But the relationship's texture is changed by what Shael knows now. And Daekin's optimism provokes them.

"Natum is dead," Shael says. "You yourself were made an outcast. So many of the people who take refuge in this house are still frightened, broken when they leave. What if struggle just isn't enough?"

"We have no choice. No alternative that doesn't make us monsters ourselves. We keep struggling with those who still have the camp in them, and we make a different world for the young. Educate them to live otherwise."

But what about the kind of people who carried the camp inside them long before the camp ever existed, Shael wonders. What if every generation includes a number of people who bear the logic of the prison in their hearts? And will inflict it on others, if given the chance?

"We'll never end the will to dominate," Daekin says, anticipating them. As if equipped with a certain intuition of the way Shael thinks. "But we can limit its power. Build social forms that don't reward it. That elevate people who are less polluted by it."

Shael watches their parent, who remains crouched, hands working the soil. "You still believe," they say, realizing it as they speak. "Even after all you've seen. All you've been through. The suffering that people who should've been your friends put you through. You still have faith that what we're doing in this place is good."

"Yes," says Daekin.

The field where Coe trains for forays isn't far from the Betweens' house, and often when Shael leaves Daekin's company they visit him there. Sometimes they train with him; mostly they just watch. Beads of sweat on his neck, lean torso shining, his small waist twisting, butt flexing as he bursts into a sprint. In hand-to-hand combat, or during target practice, Coe's body has a magnetic assurance. As if he's most himself when fighting. One day he almost kills a sparring partner. He pins the slightly older man—who has the misfortune of resembling one of the camp's worst correctors—and launches a punch towards the throat that would almost certainly be a death blow did the man not get his arm up in time to block it. There are shouts to stop the match. Comrades race over to separate the two men. "I wouldn't have connected," Coe murmurs as a dozen hands drag him back. "I would've pulled it. You know me. You know my aim. I wouldn't have connected." Gasping, the other man cradles his wrist that caught the blow. It's broken.

There's no call for a trial. Accidents happen in training all the time, and no one, including the wounded man himself, believes Coe meant to do harm. But many believe he was reckless. Shael catches whispers in the food hall. They feel the eyes of others on them differently from before: not scornful, but wary.

Of course he's like this, Shael thinks, a steady refrain that never reassures them as much as they'd like. *How could he not be like this, given the life he's led?* They feel responsible for him: their own experience of freedom—especially the struggling towards transformation that they've witnessed and practised in the Betweens' house—must now be used for Coe's benefit. No longer is it a matter of a vulnerable Between whose militant lover feels a duty to free them from camp walls; now the camp walls persist inside the militant himself, and the urgent task is to break those down. But how?

Shael hears the answer in Daekin's voice. *Walk with him. You can do no more—but also no less.*

The understanding that Coe will remain in the house in the west, will continue to sleep in Shael's bed there, becomes an accepted fact at first without discussion. Then they discuss it.

"Why should the two of them go elsewhere," Sarone says, arguing with no one.

"It's true we've found a rhythm here together," Maliez says.

They're all standing behind the house, watching Potenza play with a toy hoop, tossing it away with a flick of her wrist so it rolls back. It's mid-afternoon, the sun hanging behind clouds, no one else in sight.

"We seem to be able to live together peacefully," Coe says.

"Though we don't want to cause discomfort if you feel the house is too crowded," Shael adds.

"Stay," Potenza insists, not lifting her attention from her toy. "We would miss you too much."

Only Abia remains quiet. Uncharacteristically. She looks distracted, meets none of their eyes.

"We can keep the question open," says Maliez, watching Abia. "You had a life established before we arrived...it'd be fair if at some point you want to return to that simpler arrangement."

Abia's gaze tracks the path of Potenza's hoop, back and forth. "You're all welcome here," she says at last. "We're glad to have you with us." Almost but not quite the settlement's customary expression of hospitality and solidarity: *To be with you here is a pleasure.*

Shael notices the discrepancy. But before they can reflect on it, Coe intercepts Potenza's hoop and dashes off with it, his eyes bright with mischief. She gives frantic chase.

In the days that follow, as Shael watches more carefully how the members of the household share space, they begin to suspect the tension emanating from Abia has something to do with Coe in particular. It never crests into open conflict, but Shael observes a certain tightening in her demeanour when he enters the room, how she speaks less freely in his presence. How she studies him. At first they wonder whether they're witnessing a sexual attraction: Coe and Abia share an edge of independence that's distinctive even in this community of rebellion. But there's also a curtness to her replies when she speaks to him, a note of irritation, almost defiance. Shael is hesitant to ask either of them what's going on; the house seems peaceful, and they don't want to disrupt the peace. But they keep watching.

In the evenings, often they sit in the food hall with Calla, recently returned to Riverwish. Reclining in her wheelchair, she's more reserved than she was. It's as if she's still a little stunned by what happened on the plains, or humbled by the advanced medical technology and comforts available to support her in her convalescence. As if she's ashamed of her access to those supports, Shael thinks, though that doesn't entirely make sense to them: it wasn't Calla's mountain origins that afforded her that care; it seems likely that any comrade Hans brought to Martina's house would've received the same treatment. But maybe a complicated mood descended on her as she stayed in the mountains after the others had returned to the camp. That she could just do that, if she needed to, or chose to. That maybe, if she wanted, she would be permitted to stay there for the rest of her life—rejoin her kin—unlike the former camp participants in Riverwish, to whose fate this mountain girl had ostensibly tied her own. When she spends time with Shael now, she seldom meets their eye. They want to reassure her, let her know they believe her motives are true. She's doing what she can; she shouldn't be faulted for her origins. Look at how much she's sacrificed. But they struggle to find words, perhaps blocked by their own guilt at the memory of how readily they let themselves imagine the worst of her. That she could be a spy, a corrector in comrades' clothing.

The community is in the process of excavating a ramp down to the food hall, but in the meantime Calla needs assistance to get in and out. Usually she looks more or less at ease in her wheelchair, not visibly frustrated by her increased dependence on others. But it troubles Shael. They keep replaying in their mind the moment when those in the camp transport opened fire and wounded her. When Shael was obliged to fire back, and they killed a person. While they can't tell whether they were changed by that act in some fundamental way—the fact that they feel perhaps unchanged is disturbing to them in itself—their breath grows shallow with anger whenever those events intrude on their thoughts. How intolerable that they were put in that position, forced to take a life to save their own. Did the camp transport's defenders attack them in spontaneous self-defence? Or had the settlement's many enemies in the camp—not only its allies among the guards—been alerted that they were coming? Warned by someone in Riverwish. Someone who continues to live among them, share meals with comrades, sit in the council chamber and pass judgment on the trespasses of others.

One evening, in the food hall with Calla, Shael mentions the strain they've observed between Coe and Abia. "She's mistrustful of militants," Calla says, prodding the remains of her cake with her fork. "Thinks we're arrogant. He's certainly a militant...maybe it's no more than that." She speaks with an air of abstraction that feels loaded. It makes Shael's stomach churn.

"Do you think it's no more than that?" they ask.

"It'd be uncomradely of me to speculate," she says.

That night, Shael waits for Coe at training and accompanies him home. They walk mostly in silence. They've begun their descent into the ravine by the time Shael finds the courage to broach the subject. More nervous than they can account for.

"Can I ask you something," Shael says, and Coe stops at once, turning to them with an expression that suggests the opposite of surprise. There's no light nearby besides the glow of the moon, full and bright. More than enough to reveal the flash of Coe's eyes. "Does Abia have misgivings towards you? Did you quarrel?"

"We didn't quarrel." He pauses for a moment. "But she has misgivings."

"Are you...I mean, do you want each other?"

Coe raises an eyebrow.

"So...?"

"It struck me as strange that we were sending her sculptures to the camp."

The chill begins in Shael's scalp and inches its way down the length of their body.

"When I was in there, more or less the only objects that flowed into the camp from the settlement were documents. Information. Occasionally, when the risk seemed justified, weapons. Never art. But one of my comrades at training mentioned these beautiful wooden sculptures that had sometimes been travelling to the camp alongside our dispatches, supposedly as gifts for the daughter of a certain guard we'd turned. It made some sense to me: obviously our relations with sympathetic guards have always hinged on gifts and favours. But out of idle curiosity, I asked him whether he knew the guard's location, assignment, number. He did. It was a guard I'd turned myself. His daughter is dead."

Shael feels dizzy, as if the sides of the ravine are shifting.

Coe just looks tired. "I was pretty convinced at that point, but I needed to be sure. As soon as I had the house to myself, I broke open two of the finished sculptures. Nothing. Wood. I went into a compartment beneath her desk and smashed a third sculpture, just in case. A little scroll fell onto the floor. I picked it up and read details of the next foray we had planned—now postponed. It was all there: date, time, tactics. Personnel." His voice trembles. "Do you understand? We've been sharing our days with her and her partner. Caring for her child. Yet she knew I was supposed to be on that foray—*and she put my name on a list.*"

Shael can hardly speak. "Does she know you know?"

"I pocketed the scroll and hid the remains of the sculptures near the training field, but probably she's noticed they're missing. And that they've gone missing in the time since I arrived."

"What will you do?"

Coe says nothing.

"Think of the child," Shael says, their voice faint.

Coe is silent.

"They have processes here," Shael says. "When a wrong is done."

"This isn't just any wrong. How many comrades have been wounded or killed on forays in the past year?"

They picture the rounded stump of Calla's leg. How she winces sometimes as they help her down the stairs to the food hall. "Abia…has been kind to me," they say, barely. "Even before you arrived, she gave me a home here, I'd never known anything like it—"

"*She put my name on a list.*"

Shael feels the rage in Coe's voice like an electric shock pulsing through their chest. They gaze across the ravine, past where the land rises again: faintly, a spot of amber, the house can be seen.

"If we confronted her with the evidence. If we spoke to her."

"She'd deny, she'd claim someone else had planted the scroll, and she'd find another way to carry on with her deadly work."

"Why...when she's one of us, she grew up in the camp, she knows what it is...why, why would she..."

"Only she can say." His eyes harden with contempt. "But really. A person willing to maintain friendly relations with Magent? I see no reason why she wouldn't also make a deal with Flint. If you're open to bargaining with monstrosities, why stop at one?"

A gun aimed at them by a person in a corrector's uniform, in the chaos of a dust storm.

"How could she," they say, almost a whisper.

"You trust too easily."

"We could go to the Betweens' house. If you'd rather not stay where she is."

"Not yet. I don't want to alert her further until I've decided what to do. For now we give nothing away."

At the bottom of the ravine, the house where Shael spoke with Lea, the Magent executive, glows with pale light. Shael's gaze lingers on it as they pass by. They remember the day they first saw this house, what Maliez said then about Riverwish's conditions of possibility: *The power games that allow this place to survive are almost unmappable.* They wonder whether Maliez might suspect what Abia has been up to. Whether anyone knows about her treachery. Sarone, even Potenza...are they a whole family of spies? Or has Abia dwelt alone in her secret?

The wind moans, kicks up dust as they emerge on the ravine's far side. No light interrupts the darkness besides the glow of the house. When they reach it, Shael senses no movement within. At first they think it may be empty—very unusual after nightfall. But as soon as they and Coe step inside, they hear noises down the hall. Low voices. A sudden wail. They find Sarone, Maliez, and Potenza in Abia's workshop. The room in disarray. Sculptures split, in fragments. Those that remain intact, ranged along the edges of the room, appear to be watching the scene unfold. Sarone's weeping is mostly silent, and terrible. Maliez murmurs to Potenza, seems to be trying to offer comfort. The child's expression is grave, without tears.

"Where is she," Coe says.

Maliez strokes Potenza's hair. Her hands shake.

"At the Betweens' house," she says. "For safety before her trial."

THE QUALITY OF SILENCE THAT HANGS OVER THE council chamber is unlike any Shael has encountered before. It's as if the hundreds of people gathered are holding their breath. Dorota presides.

"We take the rare step of escalating to a Second Process without a First." If she's uneasy about the violence latent in those words, she gives no sign of it. Her hands steady, she smooths the folds of her robe. "This tribunal is invested with the power of life and death."

As at Natum's trial, rings of chairs ebb from the central circle. Potenza sits between Sarone and Maliez in the front row, across the circle from Abia. The child was told she would be welcome at the trial and also free not to attend. She insisted on accompanying the adults, though her allegiances are unclear. It would seem natural for her to support her parent despite everything, to plead for her parent's life for her own sake. But she's said little. When she does speak, mostly it's to ask questions. *Were there other lies? Or just the big one? Why would she put the messages inside the animals if she knew they would hurt people?*

"We'll hear the testimonies of those affected by this betrayal," Dorota says. And to Abia: "You don't contest that description of your behaviour? Or the details of the claims made against you?"

"I don't contest," Abia says softly.

Whispers course through the room. Abia shrinks in her seat. She looks frailer than before, almost gaunt. She makes little eye contact, though Shael sees her steal glances at her kin.

The sister of a young comrade killed in a foray stands to speak. It was an ambush, she says. A swarm of Flint's spiders surrounded her brother's vehicle before it had even crossed into the plains. "They came shockingly close to the settlement," she says. "Brazen. As if to warn us they might one day roll all the way in here, with the full horror of their war machines." Her brother's body disappeared—likely taken back to the camp for assessment—as did the bodies of those who died with him, all but one member of his foray team. "They were well-trained. All of them would be alive today if the precise details of their mission hadn't been handed over to our enemies." Mouth pinched with rage and grief, she glares at Abia. "Shame on you."

There are others. A small child who lost his mother in an ambush. A Between whose lover was murdered the same way. A food-hall coordinator who describes how Riverwish's stock of food has waned dangerously, as so many supply missions have been intercepted. Calla, who, in silence, rolls forward in her wheelchair and extends the stump of her leg. Abia absorbs this flood of pain with apparent equanimity, or numbness, while Sarone lapses into silent sobs. Potenza seems startled by each new detail, her eyes wide, wider. Not distraught, or not obviously so, but *fascinated*: how can her soft-spoken parent have been responsible for all this misery? Shael, too, reels as more of the suffering caused by Abia's deception is disclosed. An unassuming person, devoted to her close ones, able to lose herself for hours in her art: how could she have done what she did?

"Will you speak in your defence?" Dorota asks, voice tremulous with an anger that even she, with her studied poise, can't hide.

"Not in my defence," says Abia after a moment. "But I can tell you why."

"*Why*," Dorota repeats.

"Yes. Why."

Murmurs. Shifting in seats. Potenza doesn't take her eyes from her parent. Nobody does.

"I liked my life," Abia says.

The silence in the room is total.

"I liked my life, and I didn't want you all to wreck it. And you would've, if you'd kept insisting on escalating. Militants' provocations scrawled on raided transports. All your idle, boastful talk about seizing the camp. You would've eventually brought terrible repression upon us. We'd have lost everything."

"And those who lost their lives because of you!" yells a man from the back row of chairs. "They may have liked their lives as well, have you considered!"

A peal of yells, less coherent, is uncapped by the first.

"Quiet!" says Dorota.

The room hushes.

Abia hesitates. She draws a deliberate breath, releases it. "I was a militant. I'm familiar with that life. But my experiences taught me that we exist here in a fragile equilibrium. We owe our every peaceful moment to the pause in hostilities between the two beasts. That pause is our airlock dome. It keeps out toxins. Magent protects us—"

"Traitor!" someone yells, but the crowd doesn't take it up.

"Magent protects us for now, but only because Flint's power restrains it. If we were eventually to succeed in overthrowing Flint, Magent would slaughter us all before we saw the next sunrise. It would have no more use for us."

She pauses. Scans the room. Lingers on Coe, who doesn't meet her eye.

"We *cannot*," she continues, "wage a revolutionary struggle against both Flint and Magent. That's what success would require, the second front would open as soon as the first were won, and we're simply not strong enough. It's impossible to imagine how we could become strong enough. But there's so much life to live in this pause. In this breath. So much goodness. I felt it was my duty to help us keep that."

"By sending your comrades to their deaths," Dorota says.

"By providing intelligence that would keep the two beasts on an equal footing. By ensuring neither could seize a decisive advantage. To protect us all. I didn't want any comrades to die. Most of the information I relayed put no one in danger. And I did my best to subtly falsify any information that would place others in danger, to give comrades a chance. I was far from the only source of intelligence Flint has, you know. We're all familiar with the drones. It's not right to blame me for every successful trap Flint has laid. But…" She hesitates. "When my contact in the camp, a guard who'd once protected me…when he whispered to me on a foray that Flint was growing nervous about how many guards we'd organized, that they were planning to escalate hostilities against us…I felt I needed to do my part to calm the situation. Reassure Flint we posed no threat."

"You should've brought the matter to the collective," Dorota says. "We would have discussed it together and decided what to do."

"I was afraid you'd embrace the conflict. The hotheads among you. You might've even seen Flint's escalation as the moment to try for insurrection in the camp, *now or never*. Which I knew had to end badly. Suicidally, for all of us. I didn't trust you with the decision." Murmurs ripple around her. "All I wanted was to help secure a time of relative peace that might last long enough for my child to grow old in it."

Potenza seems to sense the eyes of the room falling on her. Her nose twitches. At first she doesn't move, says nothing. Then: "I…"

Sarone nods at her. So does Dorota, who says, "You are welcome." Abia stares at her, eyes leaden.

"I want to grow old," Potenza says. "But…what about the children in the camp? We can't just…leave them there."

"No," Abia says, her voice thick. "We can't."

"How can I…I don't even *want* to be happy…while there are other children trapped there. I want to be sad and angry for them every day. Until they're free."

· Tears roll down Sarone's cheeks.

"The truth is," Abia says to her child, "I didn't care about those other children as much as I care about you. I still don't."

"*Why not!*"

"Because I'm small. Because I have only so much energy. Because I'd rather care well for one person, or a few people, than care uselessly for a multitude."

"No! I don't like that!" Potenza's high, bright voice echoes.

"I'm sorry."

"I'll go into the camp! I'll put myself in a cage! Then you'll have to care about us! *Us!* All the children! If I join them, you'll have to care about freeing us all!"

Though now broken by tears and hiccups, Potenza's voice is clear, the sharpest of blades splitting the silence of the room.

"You're better than I am," Abia says. "I've always told you that. You want the best for everyone. I just wanted us to survive."

"Repent of it," Sarone says, her voice low and intense, feverish. "Beg their forgiveness, say you were wrong. It's not too late."

"It is," Abia says.

"It's not, it can't be. Ask them to let you live."

"I did what I did. They've called a Second Process. What am I to say?"

"If they, if *we* kill you, we're no better than the worst correctors in the camp." Possessed of a sudden ferocity, Sarone turns to face those seated behind her. "If you kill her, you're no better than the most vicious correctors in the camp."

"She took life first," says a soft voice.

"Indirectly," Sarone says. "Without intent."

"How could we trust her again?" says Dorota. She turns to Abia: "That's the question before us. Since you've shown yourself able to rise against us, and not even impulsively but with consideration, in cold blood."

"I don't know how you could trust me," Abia says. "I'd like to live. I value my life. But I won't grovel before you. I did what I thought was best for all of us."

"On your own." Calla's voice is calm and clear. "Without consulting the rest of us. Working *against* us. While you pretended to be living quietly, harmlessly in the west."

"You've been waiting for this moment a long time," Abia says, her flat affect lapsing into contempt.

"No," says Calla. "I've been waiting for you to stop stoking useless antagonisms, separatisms, *and join the rest of us*. Make something with us. Fight with us."

"Too late for that," Abia says. "You'd never trust me to fight alongside you now."

"Maybe not. But don't say you weren't invited. Over and over."

"Excuse me," Sarone says, her voice hardening. "We've agreed that a Second Process is to be invoked only in cases where someone is remorselessly doing violence. Where every alternative has been exhausted. That *does not* describe this case. Abia had *never* been confronted about her behaviour prior to this process. She's been given no opportunity to make amends, to change. You say this Second Process is justified by the severity of the betrayal. But the longer I sit here, the less I believe you. I think you're just vengeful. You would be killing my partner for the sake of revenge. And that would be a crime against *me*. Do you hear? I ask you. Do I not have rights in this process? Does our child not? You threaten to harm us, too."

"And you are consulted," says Dorota. "You're present."

"But without the power to stop your violence. Because we're her intimates."

"If intimates had the power to stop a Second Process, none would ever be conducted."

"Then maybe none should be conducted."

"They're necessary. At other times, you too have recognized this."

"I've *always* found your trials suspect," Sarone says, eyes flashing with rage. "So has she. So have all of us in the west. We keep apart because *we do not trust your justice*. I didn't know she was hiding messages in her sculptures, I would've stopped her if I'd known, but I won't lie to you and say I can't understand why she wanted to check your power. Why she didn't want to see you all try to overthrow the camp. She was terrified that if somehow you succeeded, if the beast from the south didn't crush you immediately, you'd be just as bad as Flint. You'd inflict your Second Processes on all who crossed you. And who would stop you."

Murmurs, growing louder, spread through the assembly.

"Your words are incoherent," says Hans, seated behind Abia. "Riverwish is *us*. This tribunal is *you*. The power you want to check is your own."

"You say as much," Sarone replies levelly, "but we all know that's a pretense. Why do certain voices dominate in this chamber? Why does *she* so often lead?" She faces Dorota, who stares back at her, unblinking. "Why do we hear so frequently from you Mountainers, relative to your numbers? And so seldom from Betweens?"

"They support the process in other ways," says Dorota.

"You drape them in honour so you don't have to grant them any actual power," says Sarone. "When has a Between led a process in this space?"

"Bradoch presided over several."

"Two. Both concerning others like them. Please. If you were honest, you'd admit that authority in our community seldom falls to those comrades, regardless of what they might have to offer. And that authority here is tied to militancy. It accrues to men, Mountainers, and women without many personal caregiving responsibilities. And it selects for certain personalities. Ruthless. Inclined to escalate to a Second Process against *someone who poses no ongoing threat*."

"You can't know that!" calls a woman from the back row. "You're her intimate, of course you want to think well of her!"

"Why shouldn't militants lead a militant community?"

Coe's tone is mild. Uncannily so.

"I accept much of what you say," he goes on. "Informality of roles is dangerous. A command structure should be clarified. But why shouldn't militants have authority? When we're the reason the settlement exists, and the reason it survives. We assume more risks. You call us ruthless, but without the realism and courage of militants, everyone here would still be in the camp."

Sarone stares at him, shakes her head. "We gave you a home."

"I'm grateful for it."

"You would kill her. She opened our doors to you, and you wouldn't hesitate to cut her throat. In the name of the collective. Of your *militancy*."

"Blame me if you'd like, but I didn't turn her in."

"No, I turned myself in," Abia says.

A tissue of whispers flutters around the room. And at once Shael guesses who smashed the sculptures in Abia's workshop: not members of the community in search of proof, but Abia herself—in despair.

"I turned myself in because I knew you knew." She speaks to Coe. "And I didn't trust you not to inflict your private justice on me. Better to throw myself on the mercy of the collective than leave myself to a man like you."

"A man like what exactly?" he asks.

"Who considers himself a hardened revolutionary. And wants to prove it. In a community where that's a road to power."

"You insult my character, but you're the one who was passing our secrets to the camp."

"To keep people like you from putting us all in danger."

"Because I want to liberate the camp? Your own daughter wants the same."

"So let her lead."

"She will, in time. But we don't have the luxury of waiting for her to come of age. We need to be fighting back now."

"You would shoot your own comrades if they refused to fight. I've known men like you all my life. You would execute your own lover if they undermined the cause."

"These are terrible accusations," Coe says. "I've done nothing to deserve them."

Shael also feels that Abia is speculating beyond what she can possibly know of him. But not beyond what Shael knows. Yes, he could shoot comrades who betrayed him. He's implied as much. *Your friends are those who stand with you,* he told them once, during a languid hour in the abandoned infirmary wing. *Your enemies are those who don't. It's a simple matter of position. And it can change in a blink.* Shael doesn't believe he would execute them, his lover, for any reason; they feel sure he'd exempt them from his rigours. But maybe they're sentimental to think so. Maybe for people like Coe, love creates no exceptions.

"You didn't turn me in, it's true," Abia says. "But who insisted on immediate escalation to a Second Process? You had no voice in that?"

At first Coe's expression is impassive. Then his mouth grows taut. "I don't like traitors."

Shael stares at him, startled.

"Vengeance," Sarone says. "You want vengeance. This trial is driven by the lowest instincts of the lowest among you."

"You arrived not long ago," Abia says to Coe, "and already you're dominating. You think you're advocating for militant discipline, but the simple truth is that you're poisoned by the camp. It's not your fault. But you have the heart of a corrector."

"Don't speak of me that way," says Coe, not raising his voice.

"Or you'll do what."

"You shouldn't test me."

"Spoken like a corrector scenting blood." She appeals to the crowd. "Haven't we heard those words before! That tone! All of you raised in the camp, is it not familiar!"

"There's a difference," Coe says slowly, "between the sadism of the correctors and a desire for fairness, order."

"Our lives *are* orderly here," Sarone says. "And our processes for dealing with harm, for all their flaws, seek to be fair. You're new here. Try listening."

"I've listened. And I heard you harboured a traitor."

"Now he accuses me!"

"She didn't know!" Abia shouts. "Corrector! Seeking excuses to beat others! To drag more of us off for exposure in a centre court! The way we kill here, it's almost the same as in the camp, did you know? We drag the unfortunate wretch out to the plains and abandon them to sink into hallucinations, starve, roast to death. Oh, that's right, we're different, more *merciful*, we leave them with a knife in case they want to speed things up. Did you ever see a condemned participant baking in a centre court? Corrector, answer me!" He makes no reply; she leaves him little time to. "I did once, when I was a child. A Between, naked. Though by the time I saw them, they were just a heap of crimson flesh. That's what you would do to me! And to Sarone! And to anyone else who crosses you! Or maybe some of us you would just beat. The small ones, maybe."

Coe explodes out of his seat. "These accusations are unjust! She has no right to speak of me this way!"

"Sit down," Dorota says.

"Are there no consequences for slander! Is there no discipline!" He wheels around to face Abia. "You should be beaten and worse! If this community won't deal with you, you're right! I'll deal with you myself!"

The chill that has been seeping through Shael turns to ice. But they can't focus on that sensation for long, as comrades flood the space in front of them. Like it was with Natum: a human wall surrounds Coe, while an equivalent group, mostly women and Betweens, encircles Abia. The chamber echoes with a chaos of voices. For a moment there's such confusion that Shael worries the barriers between Coe and Abia have been breached, he's attacked her. But as the room settles, they see the lines have held. Coe is breathing heavily, pacing, but not challenging those who box him in. Most of Abia is concealed from view by her defenders, though she can be glimpsed through the gaps between them.

The stillness of a person seated behind Dorota catches Shael's attention: Daekin, who looks lost in thought, eyes downcast. Apparently feeling Shael's gaze on them, the elder looks up, meets their glance. The two of them stay connected in this way as the chamber grows quieter again.

Daekin offers a faint smile. "It's really a puzzle," they say.

The wryness in their voice, incongruous as it is, defuses some of the tension in the room. The cordons of protectors around Coe and Abia relax, though they don't dissolve. Dorota turns to face Daekin. She nods at them to continue. Still smiling a little, they shrug. They weren't looking for permission.

"The challenge," Daekin says, "is that clearly these two aren't well-suited to life in our kind of community." They look at Abia, at Coe, without any apparent rancour. "She wants to maintain the status quo, and she's willing to lie and sacrifice others to serve that end. His violence may never be sufficiently controlled for comrades to be safe enough around him, in part because he seems to have very little awareness of what makes him dangerous. It's difficult to walk with somebody who thinks their violence is virtuous, so sees no need to struggle against it."

"I struggle against our enemies," Coe says.

"Thank you, but it's not your turn to speak," Daekin says.

Coe bristles, his jaw hinging open and shut, but he stays silent.

"We also mustn't kill either of them, I believe," Daekin continues. "I agree that to do so would make us no better than the corporations. Maybe if it were necessary, if there were truly no choice—but to establish that necessity so incontrovertibly that we could justify killing? I don't see how we could do that. So we mustn't." Though their smile has faded, their tone remains warm. "But then what to do with these two? If we can't live with them here but mustn't kill them? Maybe what's wanted is a sort of zone apart, a space of separation, where we could send those unable to heal, incapable of aligning themselves with our values, at least enough not to be a threat. We could help them transform themselves there—or, if they prove unable to transform, we could insist they stay there indefinitely. We could provide them there with the basic necessities of life. But then we would need to build a fence around that place. Install locks. We would need to guard it. And maybe we would need some way of instilling discipline there. Beyond that, to manage such a place would consume a lot of our time and energy—so we might begin to require those we'd confined to repay us somehow, perform productive labour for our sake. We spared their lives, after all. We could just as easily have killed them."

Whispers begin to snake across the assembly again.

"You see the problem," Daekin says.

"And what do you propose?" Shael replies.

"Well, I'm not sure, but I think it's good you're asking. It really is *the* question. I don't know what to say in general, in the abstract…but in this case? She's aligned herself with the camp, so let her return to the camp, if her friends there will facilitate her re-entry. She's done Flint much service, maybe she'll even be made a guard. As for him—"

The sound that interrupts them is like thunder, ear-splitting. Shael looks up. In the moment before the darkness, it seems to them the sky is falling.

DENSE CLOUDS OF DUST HANG IN THE AIR. LIGHT streams into the council chamber: a big chunk of the roof is gone. Debris lies everywhere, wide strips of the floor buried under wood and stone. Many chairs are overturned, while others stand upright in perfect order, as if there had been no disturbance. The moans of pain are also mostly contained in discrete areas, a slender path of devastation carved across the chamber.

As soon as Shael regains enough consciousness to observe all this, a wave of nausea nearly knocks them out again. Their head throbs. Sitting up gradually, gingerly, they see all at once the pools of blood and mass of bodies. They lean over and vomit. Their stomach is almost empty. When they stop coughing, they turn to the comparatively untouched swaths of the room, search the faces of the living. Relief nearly makes them sick again as they spot, right away, faces of their household. Sarone, her arms wrapped around Potenza, the child with a vivid gash across her forehead but otherwise apparently intact. Maliez crouched in front of Potenza, comforting her. Abia still in her seat, upright, as if frozen. Daekin on their feet, Bradoch and Alodia near them, Calla seemingly unscathed in her wheelchair. That such a raid could spare everyone Shael cares about—it feels lucky, too lucky. Their relief turns to dread. When they find the courage to look again at the dead and wounded, the first face they see is Coe's.

It's as if there's no air left in the room. Their body staggers towards his body without their willing it to. Many of the other dead are those comrades who formed the protective ring around him, kept him from Abia. *The other dead*—for he is motionless. A block of stone has crushed his chest. His eyes are open. He looks innocent. Beautiful. Shael screams.

They keep screaming as arms envelop them, as Maliez draws them away. Their screams lapse into sobs. They push against Maliez without thinking. She holds them, rubs their nape, the small of their back. Their face spins back to his body, to him, a cruel magnetism: it's so painful to see him this way. But they will never again see him any other way, so how can they not stare. His lower body undamaged. His lips still as red as the blood pooling around him. They're unable to stop looking until Maliez, with Sarone's gentle but firm help, pulls them back.

They feel the world is shrouded in a fog that only the most asser-tive details are able to pierce. Howls of grief as others discover kin and friends among the dead. A woman's enraged voice, screaming at Abia: "Did you do this?! She did this! Don't let her go, she's responsible, she must pay!" Abia motionless in her seat. There's a loud buzz overhead and the survivors scramble, press themselves against the chamber's walls. No attack follows, but they seem to decide at once that they shouldn't remain here, those who can move or be moved must disperse.

The dead are left behind, for now, as most of the assembly files out of the chamber. There's no prospect of dislodging the stone that pinned Coe, not unless several of them dedicate themselves to it, a task their haste forbids. For a moment, Shael's desire to stay with him, take their chances, is almost irresistible. But when Potenza slips her hand in theirs and leads them, they don't resist. They swear they'll come back for him, clean his body and give it a proper burial in the soil of Riverwish, among comrades who died here before him, far from the incinerators of the camp. But for now they must seek safety among the living.

"Did they know we were all here?" Potenza asks, as they leave the council chamber.

Shael turns to Sarone. She looks exhausted. Haunted. No one answers Potenza's question.

Many of the survivors gather in the food hall, where accusations fly. The debate is unwieldy, its terrain constantly shifting. They should have taken more security precautions for the trial of a traitor. How could they abandon the dead, they should've prioritized the dignity of the fallen above all else. Who agreed to trust the traitor's relations, they could've been accomplices. But we mustn't assign guilt by association. In a community this size? Who would escape censure? As Shael tries to keep up, they realize Dorota, one of the settlement's most practised mediators of such disagreements, is absent. When they ask Maliez whether the elder was among the dead, she responds with a grimace. Now the argument has moved on to discrepancies in care for the wounded: some of the hurt comrades are surrounded by relations, while others have just one charitable well-wisher keeping them company. A metal cup is flung against a wall. The clatter draws screams. When it's clear there's no new danger, the arguments erupt again.

Where is Abia? With a flash of panic, Shael scans for her among the other members of their household, then in the broader crowd. "I don't see her," they whisper, agitated, to Maliez. It takes Maliez a moment to understand. Her mouth tightens. She turns to Sarone. "Where is she," Maliez murmurs. Others in the room notice their distress, guess its source. "Did she escape?" "She's still in the council chamber, we need to go back for her!" "Who was watching her?" Serious but impassive, Potenza observes the community in turmoil over her parent. How must it affect her, to hear Abia become pure objectified pronoun in the mouths of the others? The indignity of the punitive control that the collective now claims over her parent, combined with the horror of discovering her parent to have been a traitor—Shael wants to shield her from it. Knows they can't.

A holler, above the buzz of voices: "Outside!" The crowd floods from the hall. Shael lingers in the rear, drifts along with Maliez and the others of their household. What could be worth rushing towards, now that Coe is dead? When they emerge into daylight, they see the crowd has assembled in a rough circle. At its centre, a broad margin of space on every side of her, is Abia. A gun cradled in her arms, as if it's a delicate creature she's nursing back to health. She doesn't look prepared to use it, though neither does she seem ready to relinquish it. Daekin is at the front of the crowd, speaking to her. Shael freezes at the sight. They can't lose somebody else today.

"I won't harm anyone," Abia says, listless. "Except myself. If you're just going to kill me regardless."

"We don't want to kill you," Daekin says.

Murmurs of dissent are audible from the crowd.

"*You* may not want to," she says. "But others do."

"I'll protect you," Daekin says. "You did me a kindness. You cared for those I care for. I won't let harm come to you."

"I believe you're sincere, but you can't promise that. There are too many here who'd consider it a service to the community to take my life. I could never sleep in this place without locks."

"Remember the suggestion I made at your trial?" Daekin says, their voice wavering as Abia adjusts her grip on the gun. "It seems likely you'd be welcome in the camp. Or at least your chances of survival there would be as great as here. I can guarantee your safety till a transport is arranged."

"And if it turns out to be a trick? If the transport just takes me to the plains to abandon me there? I'd rather die here, on my own terms."

"*No!*"

Potenza pushes her way forward. Crying, she stops right in front of Abia, who hesitates, rocks from side to side.

"I can't stay with you anymore," Abia says, her voice dull, flat. As if she's already far away. "I'm sorry. It would make you too unsafe."

"Will you be safe in the camp?"

"I don't know. If I could actually get there. If they'd let me. Maybe I'd be safer there than here. And certainly you'd be safer than if I were to remain in this place."

"Then go," Potenza says in a fierce whisper. "And wait for me there. Wait for the day I free you. I promise I will."

It's as if a string of tension had been running through the centre of Abia's body and, in an instant, has gone slack. Releasing a low moan, she crumples in place. The gun falls with a clatter. Daekin rushes over, snatches it, and stands with Abia as dozens of others press into the space around her.

"Get back!" Daekin shouts.

Startled, the others obey.

"No one lays a hand on her. I've promised her safety until we can convey her onward. You all have heard me. You will not make a liar of me."

The grumbles from the crowd are brief and quiet. The comrades who approached Abia fall back. Still gripping the gun, Daekin meets Shael's gaze.

"Those of my household," Daekin says. "Please join us."

DESPITE

THE BETWEENS' HOUSE IS FULL. EVERY BETWEEN in Riverwish is there, it seems, drawn home by the caravan protecting Abia. Bradoch is at the piano. How can there be music in the world but not Coe? Shael can't comprehend it. How can the world just go on existing? In the wake of the day's losses, how can Alodia simply lounge on a couch in the common room, brushing their long, thick hair out of their face?

Alodia feels Shael's eyes on them, looks up. "What?"

Shael blinks. Can't find words. None that would make any sense.

A few Betweens, Daekin among them, guard the bedroom where Abia has been granted sanctuary. It's after nightfall when Daekin leaves that post to speak to Shael, half whispering in the hallway downstairs.

"You believe she's sincere about returning to the camp," Daekin says.

"She knows she can't stay here," Shael replies.

"Will you speak to her and make sure of her intentions? She trusts you."

It isn't quite the same as the struggles that Betweens in this house routinely undertake with the guilty. There's no prospect of her reintegration into the community. But as Shael sits at her bedside, navigating her fears, they feel themselves to be part of a lineage. *We have always done this. We have always been asked to do this, always been able to do this.* Not only console or counsel, but mediate between darknesses. Practice a cartography of transformation in a zone of unmarked roads. Foster the imagination of a future whose ethical foundation could be a goodness without innocence. A decency won by struggling through guilt. Not for the sake of a transcendent moral order—but for each other's sake.

"Would you come with me? On the transport?" she asks Shael.

"If you want me to."

"It would help me believe they don't mean to kill me."

Yet she'll still be headed back to the camp. Incredible, Shael thinks, how much people want to live, no matter the circumstances. Better the possibility of a life caged and humiliated than the near-certainty of death. It's such attachment to bare existence that allows the camp to persist. Coe never shared it. He refused to accept life without freedom—and so was willing to risk life for freedom. He would never, under any circumstances, have let himself be sent back to the camp. Nor would he have relinquished whatever power and influence he might have built in Riverwish; Abia had seen him clearly. He would have risen to a position of leadership, ruthlessly forging a path for himself, if he weren't first destroyed by the antagonisms he stoked in the process. What to do with such a comrade? How to keep him from slashing a community into a web of seismic rifts? The question seems to have no good answer. Shael is haunted by it. They also feel sure that without people like Coe, Riverwish wouldn't have been founded. Every person born in the camp would still be imprisoned there.

They will never stop missing him.

"It's fine if you can't forgive me," Abia says. "But I hope someday you do."

They aren't angry with her. They feel, again, that they understand her all too well—the lengths to which a person might go for a chance at just a few more idle, pleasant years. But they aren't sure whether that understanding is the same as forgiveness.

"I'm grateful for the home you gave me," they say. "And I promise I'll always protect the others there, as well as I can."

She holds their gaze for a long time, her expression unchanging, inscrutable. "Thank you."

In the house in the west, life feels muted without Abia and Coe. It's a hush produced not only by the absence of those voices: Potenza, too, says less, and the remaining adults speak more softly than they did, mourning without ritual. There has been talk of a ceremony to honour all those lost in the attack, but no one has yet taken the initiative to organize it. The shock and pain are too fresh, the losses too many, touching all those who survived. There's a widespread sense of disorganization, inertia. Also a diffuse feeling that Riverwish's informal core of leadership has shifted to the Betweens' house, the Between elders now steering everyone through crisis. Daekin and Bradoch, especially, are seen in the centre of the settlement more than ever. They spend hours in the food hall and walking in the long shadows of the town's ruins, conferring with comrades. But when Shael asks Daekin what comes next, how their community might rebuild, the elder says only: "We'll see."

Supplies flow into Riverwish without disruption. The community's stock of food is replenished. Forays run smoothly. "My eternal thanks to your man for making my job so much easier," Hans says to Shael as they dine together in the food hall. Calla, down the table from them, invites Shael to visit her more often. "I didn't mean to be aloof," she says. "But when you joined her household, I felt I needed to step back. Not that I knew the half of it! It's interesting how those who affect to be purer and less compromised than everyone else so often have a lot to hide."

Abia hasn't left her refuge. Shael visits her there, sits with her, assures her that the plan is still to convey her back to the camp once the necessary arrangements have been made. Otherwise neither of them has much to say. One night, Shael descends from Abia's room and sees Daekin blocking the house's front doorway. Just outside is Lea, the Magent executive. A silent standoff ends as Shael draws near: Lea stalks away, disappearing into the darkness. Perplexed, Shael turns to Daekin. "She wanted to take possession of our guest," Daekin says. "But she has no authority here." A shiver runs through Shael. "They have *no* authority here," Daekin repeats, their voice rising, tremulous. "This is *our house.*"

Nevertheless, Magent's interest in Abia accelerates the plan to get her out. Comrades in the camp have located the guard who was tasked with processing her dispatches. At first he's unwilling to help, but the comrades have leverage over him—proof he's been falsifying work logs to help his lover, a participant—and before long he's more co-operative, promises to work with a sympathetic assessor to reintegrate Abia quietly into the camp's databases, in recognition of the difficult, important service she's rendered. She's to be snuck onto a camp transport and resurrected in captivity. Strange to hope for that outcome, Shael feels, bleak as it is. But they do.

Without having been told, Potenza seems to know that her parent's departure is imminent. One afternoon, Shael comes across her standing motionless in Abia's old workshop. The room is otherwise empty now, the last of the sculptures cleared out. "I won't be able to visit her there," Potenza says. "It's so strange. If I were to visit, they would trap me. What kind of place is that?"

Shael has no idea how to respond. "Like you said, one day we'll free them all," they venture, not entirely convincing themselves.

"Yes, of course," Potenza says, as if the inevitability of liberation is the plainest common sense. "But until then, I can't visit? It's strange." She begins to shake. Shael opens their arms to her, and she steps into their embrace. "What we need," she murmurs, "is many settlements. The problem is that we have only Riverwish. So she has to go back to the camp, because there aren't other options. There should be a hundred settlements, each with its own ways. Then she could simply go to another. If they'd take her." Shael looks at her, astonished. She buries her face in their stomach, grips them tighter. "And then I could visit," she whispers.

The day when Shael escorts Abia from Riverwish is otherwise unremarkable. Shael sets out in the early morning and is back before dark. Upon their return to the house in the west, they're asked little and say less, except to confirm that she was safely removed from the settlement's transport to the camp's. That she sent her love again as she left, repeating what she'd told the others of her household when they'd visited her refuge before her departure: she would always miss them and hope for their happiness. When more time has passed, maybe Shael will also share what Abia said next, as she descended to the plains, the sun hot on their faces: that she was sorry for the pain she'd caused, but would do the same again tomorrow if she thought it might protect those she loved. Dust swirled between the two vehicles as the camp transport remained paused at its planned stop. Their guard had left the hold unlocked. She had to run now, while there was still time. None of them knew what might happen if the attempt to evacuate her failed—how the community might respond. Daekin could protect her for only so long. "Go," Shael said, and watched as she did, not looking away until the dust had drawn its curtain around her.

Her departure doesn't break the new tension in Riverwish. The loss of life from the raid still feels shocking, not quite real and too real, as does the raid itself—the escalation it represents. The community may never know whether Abia somehow alerted Flint to the trial's timing. She denied it, and Shael considers it unlikely: they don't believe she would have knowingly put Sarone's and Potenza's lives at risk. But however the raid came about, Flint's willingness to target the settlement's population so brazenly, bomb the council chamber in the middle of the day, feels like a dangerous new state of affairs. Assuming it was Flint.

Could it have been you? they wonder when they see Lea. She greets them with the same remote civility as ever—until the morning when they pass her as they're crossing the ravine, and she fixes her intense eyes on them and says: "If your people ever want revenge, come speak with us."

They stop. Stare. "Why would you help us?"

She's been walking along the edge of the railway tracks, a small black box in her hands. Now she glances at the box, flips a switch on it, and slides it into a pocket of her robe. "Magent is in the process of reviewing whether we consider that vicious attack a breach of our treaty. We're divided on the question. But if we conclude the treaty was broken, everything will change. And you may find it prudent to deepen your friendship with us."

Her gaze sends ice through them, but they don't look away.

"Give it some thought," she says. And she turns and walks towards her house.

They want to ask Daekin about what she told them. Her invitation. But each time they consider broaching the subject, Daekin strikes them as stressed, exhausted. Everyone brings their problems to the elder now. Finally, one evening, dusk falling around the two of them in the garden by the Betweens' house, Shael asks: "What will we do if Flint keeps escalating attacks? Deepen our alliance with Magent?"

"Not if we can help it," Daekin says after a moment's hesitation, plucking weeds. "We'll make ourselves harder to trace, cluster only when necessary. Strengthen our relationships with our friends in the mountains and the camp. Movements like ours have always been difficult to crush completely. The corporations, you know, they're giants. We're a virus. And wherever we go, wherever our ideas travel, we make more of ourselves."

Speaking this way, with militant optimism, seems to tire Daekin. They lean against the garden fence.

"You brought me back," they say. "Do you know that? I hadn't attended a trial in a very long time before Natum's." Their eyes glow, sparks in the fading light. "My responsibility to my comrades, after they turned on me...felt diminished. But then you were there. And I never stopped feeling a responsibility to you."

Riverwish seems, more than ever, a delicate tissue of such personal ties of obligation, care. Comrades tend to their closest relations, sometimes expanding that circle when doing so feels possible. No other raid comes in the weeks after the disaster, nor is there intelligence of one impending. A reprieve, a chance to rebuild as best they can, though everyone seems to feel there will be no full return to the community's prior normal. Their lives will be marked by more caution, less trust; they'll more often scan the skies and each other for signs of danger. But they'll make do. They have no choice, and they have no choice together. Their settlement of the jailbroken is, more than ever, an independence that tastes like constraint. But in that constraint are, as ever, pockets of freedom. Joyful despite.

Despite, say, the ease with which Abia's intimates could each sink into their private grief. Maliez and Sarone, Shael and Potenza—all would have warrant to. But the adults seem to sense this would be a betrayal of the child, who often appears uncannily calm but will weep for hours over a small stain on her robe. For her sake, the others try to rally, or at least not succumb altogether to despair. Maliez is experienced with this kind of discipline—she speaks of her son, abducted by Flint, more and more often—and helps them along. She delegates, organizes: the preparation of their meals, the laundering of their clothes, even the hours of their sleep. All of them remain devoted to Potenza's education. Together they read and discuss books from before the time of the camp, as well as Mountainers' texts exploring languages, mathematics, the natural world and its technological extensions. Histories official and unofficial. They keep their bodies active. Stay in motion.

In the early evenings, sometimes, when the day's heat has tapered but the sky is still light, they ride their bicycles across the field by the house. Sometimes they ride even farther west, away from the ravine where the railway glints. Farther west there's almost nothing, just open sky and sun-baked desolation. Shael knows, they have seen maps, they have heard from trusted comrades that if they were to journey far enough in that direction, following the road that presses west then curves towards the south, eventually they'd reach zones of more intense heat and contamination, the toxic wreckage of old conflicts littering the landscape like steel flowers. Maybe they would become too weak to continue cycling, temperatures soaring beyond what the human body can endure. But if they were to preserve one last access of strength and keep going, they imagine they might begin to catch the scent of salt water. They might arrive at the first dunes and, faltering, but sensing the heave of blue beyond the hills, press on. They might survive just long enough to see it.

ACKNOWLEDGEMENTS

Thanks to Saima Desai for reading an early version of *Disobedience*, talking to me about it, and eventually acting as a consulting editor on one of the final drafts. Working with you when you were editing *Briarpatch Magazine* taught me so much; you should edit a lot more magazines and books, in my opinion.

John Elizabeth Stintzi, I feel so lucky that we became pals on Twitter like seven years ago. Your example helped me understand parts of my consciousness for which I didn't yet have adequate language, showed me possibilities for doing gender in ways that felt better. It can be trite to talk about transfem bravery, but witnessing your courage was a big deal for me! Thanks a lot. I'm honoured that you agreed to edit this book, and grateful that you edited it with such care.

Thank you to Stephanie Sinclair, Mirka Loiselle, Selena Hofmann, Saima Desai (again), Jonathan Brown Gilbert, AGA Wilmot, Kirah Hahn, and Hayleigh Wronski for reading drafts of *Disobedience* and sharing helpful feedback. Extra giant thanks to Stephanie Sinclair for championing the novel, first at Transatlantic Agency and later at CookeMcDermid, and to

Evan Brown at Transatlantic for a set of brilliant notes. Charlene Chow, a million thanks for believing in this book when it landed at Book*hug Press, and for your spot-on insights into how it could be improved. Jay MillAr and Hazel Millar of Book*hug, thanks deeply and always for going to bat for literary experiments, including mine, and for all your generosity and care.

Huge appreciation also for the support of the Canada Council for the Arts and the Ontario Arts Council, which funded the development of this novel through their Explore and Create and Recommender Grants for Writers programs, respectively. Thanks to Book*hug Press for recommending *Disobedience* for support through the latter program.

Gratitude to all the community organizers and revolutionaries, especially those rooted in the Black feminist tradition, who teach us what abolitionist practices can look like today and what they might flower into tomorrow: who articulate, in the radical geographer Ruth Wilson Gilmore's words, abolitionist politics as "small c communism without a party." Thanks to Ursula K. Le Guin, obviously, and to Octavia E. Butler and all her spiritual descendants, those worldmaking visionaries who work to forge a rich relationship between literary production and social movement organizing. Thanks to the queer elders and ancestors who invented flagging. Gratitude to the many Indigenous nations of the territory on which I dwell, who teach us, through their endurance and resurgence, that white colonial lifeways—and all their repressive infrastructures—are not inevitable: alternatives have long existed.

Thanks to my sibling, Adam, and to my parents, Roz and Lorne.

Thanks to my comrades, actual and potential. This book is for you.

ABOUT THE AUTHOR

DANIEL SARAH KARASIK

DANIEL SARAH KARASIK (they/them) is the author of six previous books, including two poetry collections, *Plenitude* and *Hungry*, and the short story collection *Faithful and Other Stories*. Their work has been recognized with the Toronto Arts Foundation's Emerging Artist Award, the CBC Short Story Prize, and the Canadian Jewish Playwriting Award. They've organized with the network Artists for Climate & Migrant Justice and Indigenous Sovereignty (ACMJIS), among other groups, and are the founding managing editor of *Midnight Sun*, a magazine of socialist strategy, analysis, and culture. They live in Toronto.

Colophon

Manufactured as the first edition of
Disobedience
in the spring of 2024 by Book*hug Press

Edited for the press by John Elizabeth Stintzi
Editorial consultation by Saima Desai
Copy-edited by Stuart Ross
Proofread by Laurie Siblock
Type + design by Michel Vrana

Printed in Canada
bookhugpress.ca